THE DOM'S HOSTESS

A BILLIONAIRE SECRET BABY ROMANCE - ISLAND OF LOVE SERIES BOOK 1

MICHELLE LOVE

HOT AND STEAMY ROMANCE

CONTENTS

Made in "The United States" by:

Michelle Love

© Copyright 2021

ISBN: 978-1-64808-785-1

❀ Created with Vellum

BLURB

Astor Christakos needed a vacation from the reality of being the CEO of a high-powered investment company.

Nova Blankenship had been offered a new job.
That's how they both found themselves at the newest tropical island resort opened by billionaire Galen Dunne: Nova as a hospitality hostess, Astor as an entitled guest who had to have things his way or else.
The practicing Dom hadn't met a suitable Sub in some time, and Nova could use a man's hand to smooth out her rougher edges. And so Astor's hunger began to sizzle for the young, succulent hostess. Though she protested and argued that she could not and would not be tamed by him or any man, Astor took her on as a challenge.
But who would end up owning whom in the end?

1

NOVA

I walked along the sandy white beach, watching as the crystal clear water lapped at the shore. I was on my way to an important interview, but I couldn't resist taking my time to take in the tropical beauty.

Leaving my work family at Club Contiki, the bar I'd worked at in the Florida Keys for years, wasn't something I'd ever considered before, but when you get an invitation to interview for a job at a new Caribbean resort for one of the world's most renowned billionaires, you'd be stupid to pass up that opportunity.

Galen Dunne, best known for developing cutting-edge automobile software, designing marine vessels that looked like they came straight out of a James Bond movie, and planning expeditions into space, was working on something a little different for his next project. The enigmatic billionaire now owned an island of his very own—and they were hiring.

Mrs. Chambers, the woman who'd contacted me through my work e-mail, told me they were searching for just the right people to staff this island. Galen wanted it to become a resort for the wealthiest of the wealthy, and they needed people with experience to run the place.

I'd been working as a concierge at Club Contiki for the last few years. Before that, my family had run a small resort inland. I'd grown up catering to guests. Making sure that everyone had a good time, or that they were left alone to relax—it came naturally to me. I was great at helping people achieve whatever they wanted.

When my parents retired, I looked for work in the same industry. Club Contiki took a chance on me, putting me in housekeeping at first. Their clientele—mostly celebrities—demanded they hire only people who knew how to control themselves around famous people.

Although I'd grown up catering to average people, ones with regular social status and normal jobs, I have a knack for regarding everyone for exactly what they are—human. In short, I'm not one to fawn over someone just because of their net worth or fancy career.

Treating all people with respect and judging them based on their character has been my motto. So far, it's worked in my favor. After one summer of housekeeping, I moved forward to guest services. That meant I was doing much more interesting things than simply making beds and sweeping sand off the floor.

I'd had lots of fun working at Contiki, but maybe I'd have even more fun working at this new, mysterious-sounding resort—especially because that resort happened to be in the gorgeous Caribbean.

That's why I'd accepted Mrs. Chambers's invitation and invited her to be my guest at Contiki for the weekend.

With the summer season still a few months away, there were plenty of empty suites available. One perk of working there was being able to have guests from time to time when availability afforded it.

One of the hostesses had seated Mrs. Chambers at a table near the water, making sure she had a tropical cocktail in her hand. Her blonde hair flowed behind her in the warm breeze coming off the ocean, and she looked regal as she sipped the blue cocktail from the slender glass.

"Hello, Mrs. Chambers," I greeted her with a warm smile. "I'm Nova Blankenship."

Rising to a full six-foot-something, she reached out to shake my hand. "It's a pleasure to meet you, Miss Blankenship. Thank you so much for making me your guest this weekend. I have to say that no other candidate has offered such a gesture for me throughout this interviewing process."

Motioning to the chair she'd gotten up from, I moved to take the one on the other side of the small table for two. The high bar-style chairs had my feet dangling over the sand while her long legs reached all the way to the ground where her bare feet trailed in the sand. "Please, let's sit and get to know one another."

With a nod, she picked up her drink again. "This is delicious, by the way. Thank you for having it sent to me. Is that a hint of mango I taste?"

"The bartender is a master of concoctions. He uses coconut water as the base and all sorts of tropical fruit-infused rums." I crossed my legs at the ankles, propping one foot on the bar under the chair and leaning back to take in a nice deep breath of sea air. "I would love to know more about this private island Mr. Dunne purchased."

"It's gorgeous," she said as she beamed at me. "He's a genius, as you've likely already heard. His ideas are beyond compare, and this one is no different. His plan is to establish the private resort as a haven for the world's wealthiest people." She waved her long, elegant hand through the air as she shook her head. "I've already told you that in the e-mails we've exchanged this last month. I hate to waste time saying the same old things. Don't you?"

"It bears repeating, I would think," I replied with a smile. Molly, the waitress serving our table, walked up on one side of me, capturing my attention. "Good afternoon, Molly."

"Afternoon, Nova." She smiled and nodded at my guest that she'd met earlier. "Mrs. Chambers, are you enjoying your drink?"

"I am." Mrs. Chambers took another sip. "When you get a chance, another would be great."

"Of course," Molly said before turning her attention to me. "You're not on the clock, Nova. Care for anything?"

"Why not? I've got the weekend off to spend time with my guest." I figured I could relax a bit myself. "Bring me one of the same, please, Molly."

"I'll be right back." She looked over her shoulder at me as she walked away. "Should I make a reservation for you and your guest for dinner tonight?"

I'd already made all our plans for the weekend. I wanted to let Mrs. Chambers see what I could do. "That's not necessary, Molly. I've already taken care of all the arrangements myself. Thank you for offering, though"

As Molly walked away, Mrs. Chambers's expression looked to be one of approval as she gazed at me. "I've got to tell you that I adore your style, Miss Blankenship."

"Thank you. And please, call me Nova." I didn't much care for formal names.

"Okay. Then you must call me Camilla." Reaching across the table, she placed her hand on top of mine. "I don't often ask anyone to call me by my first name."

"I'm honored." I meant that, too. I could tell the woman had a lot of credentials to back her up. I admired her already. "I've told you about my background in guest services, but what I haven't told you yet is what I want for my future. Care to hear?"

"Please." She sat up, curiosity filling her pretty face. The woman had excellent bone structure. She couldn't have been more than forty, and she'd kept herself in shape, too. "What does the future look like for you, Nova?"

Running my hand through my hair to move it out of my eyes, I looked up at the cloudless blue sky. "I love to work hard, and I adore living in paradise. I love what I do, and I want to keep moving ahead with this line of work. I want to move up and up until there's nowhere else to go. I want to take college classes and gain a degree so that I can one day earn a management position with a resort."

I thought about how I wanted to pay for my schooling and added, "I don't want to get into debt to get my degree, though. That's what I've been planning since I began working here three years ago, when I was just twenty years old. Out of every paycheck, I've put ten percent into an account to be used one day for tuition. And I would probably like to continue working as much as possible while taking classes."

"Smart." She picked up her drink and drained the last drops from it.

Molly returned with our drinks, replacing Camilla's and placing mine in front of me. "Here we go, ladies. Is there anything else I can get you two?"

"How about some lobster nachos?" I asked as I looked at Camilla.

"Sounds yummy." She licked her lips.

"Okay. Molly, an order of the nachos for two, please." Picking up my drink, I took a sip. "This is so good."

"I'll let William know that you're both enjoying the cocktails," Molly said as she turned to leave. "I'll get those nachos and be right back."

Camilla cocked one brow at me. "And when you have enough money saved to go to college, will you need to be inland to do that?"

"No, ma'am. I'm going to take online classes." I'd already researched everything and planned it all out. "I've already got the college picked out and everything. I'm just waiting on that savings account to fill up."

Camilla chewed her lower lip, seeming to think about what she wanted to ask me next. Then it popped out, "You wouldn't want to tell me what you're making now, would you?"

Moving the drink off the cocktail napkin Molly had placed it on, I pulled a pen out of my pocket and jotted my salary on it before pushing it toward her. "There it is."

"Hmm," she mused. "I can see why it's been taking you a while to get that savings account fattened. At this rate, it'll take you at least three more years." Tapping her chin with one long, pink nail, she looked deep in thought. "I can assure you that you'll have what you need before a year has passed if you take the job I've got to offer you."

"A year?" I asked with enthusiasm. I knew she was right; it would take at least another three years to save enough to start taking classes —and that was only if no emergencies came up to deplete the savings. "Okay, may I ask a few questions about this job?"

"Ask away." Camilla's eyes widened when Molly set down a

heaping platter of nachos. "Oh, my goodness. That looks and smells delicious!"

"I can promise that you won't be disappointed, Mrs. Chambers," Molly said with a grin.

Popping a lobster-covered tortilla chip into her mouth, Camilla moaned. "So good."

"Thank you, Molly," I said. "They do look especially great today."

"I'll be back to check on you ladies in just a bit. Enjoy," Molly said, then left us alone.

Ignoring the food for a moment, I asked, "What exactly would I be doing at this job?"

"You would be making sure our guests have everything they need to have an enjoyable time." She picked up another chip. "But that doesn't mean you'd have to do anything that you don't want to do."

"So, this isn't the kind of job where I'd have to accept any...positions that I might not want?" I wanted to make sure we were talking about the same thing. *Sex.*

With a nod, Camilla scooped up a good amount of the creamy lobster sauce. "Sex isn't restricted between staff and guests. That said, we won't allow our staff members to accept money or gifts in exchange for it, and we'd never ask it of them. We're only hiring adults. Our guests will mostly be adults. We understand that these things might come about naturally, but some guests may bring younger family members or friends. Obviously, underage sex is a no-no, but as far as staff and adult guest relations goes, Mr. Dunne hasn't restricted interactions between them."

"I don't like to mix business with pleasure in that regard," I let her know. "It makes for hard feelings and is bad for business in my opinion. I wouldn't be having any relations of that sort with any guest or coworker at your resort." Her description was giving me a better idea of what the job really was. "What you want is a concierge. Is that right?"

"Um," she put the sauce-laden chip into her mouth as she contemplated my question. Swallowing it down, she took a drink, then answered, "We don't want to call you by that title. We want to make things simpler. Your title would simply be hostess. You would be expected to treat everyone as your guest and make them feel welcome. It would essentially be what you're doing for me this weekend: showing me around, planning activities—whatever the guest desires. And I've got to say that you're treating me extremely well.

Nova, I think you would be perfect for this job. You're much more impressive than anyone I've interviewed so far. So, please tell me what you're thinking about all of this?"

Everything sounded great so far. "I would need to give my boss a month's notice. He'll have to find a replacement for me, and I would need to train them for at least a week or so."

Getting up from her seat, she came around the table to stand next to me. "I would love to meet this boss of yours and be at your side when you tell him that you're giving notice and coming to work at Paradise Resort as soon as he can spare you." She leaned in close to whisper the salary to me, and my head began to spin.

"Really?" I had to ask.

She laughed, throwing her head back. "Nova, things are about to change for you, my dear girl."

Excitement filtered in past the shock of being offered a great job with a salary I never would've expected. "I'm ready for that, Camilla. Count me in. Let's go see my soon-to-be ex-boss."

2

ASTOR

I gazed down into the sparkling azure waters of the Aegean Sea as I leaned against the balcony railing. Coming to my office in Athens, Greece, always feels like coming home to me. I've been traveling for business for the better part of the year, and my family was pestering me to take some time for myself. I was finally contemplating doing just that.

Mama and Papa had no idea how much time and hard work it had taken to become the wealthy man I was. At thirty-three years old, I'd probably put in more hours than most retirees. Traveling took most of my time, meetings with investors and partners negotiating deals took the rest of it.

All that work left no time for Astor to play.

In my younger years, I'd be deep in the BDSM scene, taking on submissives to help me relax after a hard day's work. After all, there was nothing like great sex to help blow off steam. But my business grew as I made more and more connections all over the world. My time became too precious to spend molding young females into prime submissive partners.

In the end, I let it all go by the wayside. The last few years had been filled with new endeavors to distract myself—one being the construction of an entirely new resort in the Caribbean. My good friend Galen Dunne, who I'd partnered with in many other business ventures, had bought himself a private island. After spending a couple of years on the island alone, he wanted to make it into a resort.

Galen wasn't like most people—few people who achieved such success were. Being a genius who could make money doing almost anything, Galen didn't want a typical tropical island resort. No, my friend wanted the best of the best. And only people with a similar lifestyle to his would be invited.

One great thing about being friends with Galen was that between he and his friends, no money would ever change hands at his resort. Instead, we traded work for our time on the island. I'd done my part by having the swimming pools and various waterscapes built for the island. Five of the most outstanding pools I'd ever designed went a long way toward making the place he'd named 'Paradise' the most beautiful place I'd ever seen. And I'd seen more than my fair share of resorts.

Marble mermaids leapt out of a cavernous waterfall to greet guests as they walked up the pathway to the main building and lobby. Other waterscapes featured a giant squid, seashells, and even a sailboat. My team of builders had done me proud by the end of the project. Galen agreed that he'd never seen such beautiful work.

It had been a few months since I'd been on the island. Once we'd finished the work, I had other things to tend to. I'd been in China after that for a little while, and now I'd finally had a chance to come home to Athens for a bit.

My parents lived in a palatial estate that I'd bought for my family after I'd secured my first huge contract. My father had made his living as a butcher in Athens, and we'd grown up in a modest home in a neighborhood full of working class families.

When I made my first million, I told him to retire and to come live in the large home I'd bought for them. They'd all gushed over the home, a six-thousand square foot masterpiece of architecture that one of my new colleagues had designed and built in his younger days. He wanted to sell it as he'd built his family a new, larger home.

When I made my first billion, I told them I wanted to sell the house they'd grown to love. Amidst the grumbling of my family, only Mama trusted me. "You all be quiet and let your brother speak. He's never let us down before. Why should we think he would now?"

When I took them to the new home, a sprawling mansion with the first swimming pool I'd ever designed right in the middle of it, they all forgot about the other home and instantly fell in love with the new one. The looks on their faces had made it all worthwhile. That's one of the reasons I worked as hard as I did.

The other reason was that I gave my everything to making money. Well, I simply loved it. I loved the excitement of making deals: haggling to get the best price, the best cut of meat, the best materials —you name it. I wanted the best of it. And I became damn good at bargaining to get the best.

It brought me so much satisfaction, being able to save money on behalf of the people I'd invested in. It made it possible for them to get the best materials they needed for their projects at the best prices. The savings always funneled back into other parts of the projects, often allowing them to do the best work of their careers.

So yes, I worked hard so I could provide for my family, but I did it for me as well. By working alongside my father at the butcher shop, I paid my way through a business degree, not wanting to burden him with the cost. As the oldest of six children, I saw it as my responsibility to help my family out—and that meant all of them.

Throughout the years, both of my brothers had married and moved their wives into the home. Nieces and nephews soon began to fill up the massive halls. My three sisters, younger than my brothers and I, waited a few years before marrying. But all of them had. And all of them had moved out to live with their husbands, letting their men provide homes for their families.

As a Greek man, I knew that my brothers-in-law had pride that would never allow me to provide for the families they'd made. But I gave my sisters and their children extravagant gifts that ensured none of them would ever do without anything they ever wanted.

I could see how happy my siblings were with their families, but I knew that that life just wasn't for me. Married to my business, I'd made peace with the fact I would never settle down and become what my brothers had grown into: loving husbands and devoted fathers.

I loved women, but most of them—other than a submissive— thought me too stern to be a suitable romantic partner. And I agreed. I didn't care about romance, didn't have time for love. And certainly no time for all that sappy love-talk I'd heard from my brothers and brothers-in-law at times.

No, that didn't come naturally to me. I'd always been a man who got to the point. If I wanted a woman, I let her know. If she didn't care for my way of speaking or acting, then she let me know fairly quickly as well. If she liked my stern ways, that was easy to determine as well.

No need to complicate things with pretty words or emotion. That's how I liked it.

As I took in a deep breath of the salty sea air, I thought about what I wanted to do next. So many projects were on the table; it was a daunting task to decide which one to go for next.

When the phone rang and I saw Galen's name on the screen, I swiped to answer his call. "Galen, hello! It's nice to hear from you."

"Glad to make your day, Astor," he spoke with an Irish accent. Being from Dublin, Galen had made quite the name for himself on the Emerald Isle he called home before moving on to the rest of the world. "I'm callin' to invite ya to Paradise. Next week we're having our first guests, and I want ya to be one of them."

"Next week?" I asked. "So soon?"

"Yes, so soon." He laughed the hearty way only he could. "Leave your business behind ya for the summer, lad. Ya deserve the break. I've got chefs comin' from all over the world to cook for us this summer. And the staff has been preparing for our arrival, too. Prepare to get pampered, my boy."

"Pampered," I echoed him. "Not something that happens too often to me, Galen." The thought of taking the entire summer off had my blood running hot with enthusiasm. "But spending the days lazing in the sun, swimming in the crystal clear waters of the Caribbean does sound pretty wonderful..."

"And invigorating," he added. "So, when can I expect to see ya?"

"I'm not sure." There were always loose ends that needed to be tied up before going anywhere. "I think my assistant has papers for me to sign and then there's a meeting I should attend in New York. I think that's in a week or two..."

"Nonsense. Tell them all you will see them in August. Your May, June, and July are taken up with other things." He let out another laugh that sounded as if it came straight from his belly. "Things like relaxing on the beach, drinking exotic potions my bartenders are coming up with as we speak, and maybe even a woman or two."

"Women?" I asked as I laughed. "I doubt I'll find anyone to have a fling with. Who else have you invited?"

"A handful of people. There will be plenty of eligible women in Paradise, you know. After all, what would paradise be without them?" he asked.

"It's been so long since I've had a fling, I don't know if I remember how to flirt." I'd never been big on flirting anyways. Flirting didn't get to the point quick enough.

"Well, the drinks will help ya with that chore, Astor the Greek. I'll make a note that I'll be seeing ya on the first day of May in Paradise. Be there or be square." He laughed at his old joke.

Even though I'd yet to decide whether I'd be going or not, the man had me laughing, something I didn't do often enough. "You know what? I think I will take you up on this offer, my Irish friend. I'll see you on the first day of May."

"I'll be waitin' for ya with a cold drink in my hand," he said. "Or, better yet, I'll have a beautiful lass waitin' for ya with a cold drink in her hand. I've given each of my esteemed friends their own personal host or hostess. And I'll pick out just the right gal for you, my friend."

"Don't go trying to be a matchmaker, Galen. And don't have any drink ready for me, either. I've given up alcohol and sugar per my personal trainer's advice." I also worried he might be offended if I refused the woman he picked out for me to use while on his island. "And I like to pick out my own women, if you don't mind."

"Oh, I don't mind a bit. You can pick out of any of them ya like. I just want to give my guests the star treatment by giving them a host or hostess to make sure they get to experience all Paradise has to offer. I don't want anyone of you to miss out on a thing. There's so much to do and see—you'll need a hostess to see to that."

He'd settled my mind, and now I felt nothing but excitement at the idea of my impending vacation. "You know what? I think this might be just what I need. Thank you, my good friend. I can't wait to get to Paradise for the summer."

3

NOVA

The day had finally come. The island's first visitors were booked to spend the summer in Paradise and would be arriving the very next day. Camilla Chambers had all the hosts and hostesses lined up, ready to receive her news of who would be taking care of which guests.

"I've got the list right here." She sorted through the stack of papers she held in her hand, but looked up as someone entered the lobby. "Mr. Dunne! Hello! What a surprise. I didn't know you'd be here today. I thought you were coming tomorrow?"

Even though I now worked at the man's island, I still found it hard to believe that Galen Dunne himself was strolling into the lobby. "Mrs. Chambers, it's nice to see ya. I wanted to get here early to greet my first guests." He scanned the line of employees, his blue eyes stopping abruptly on me. "And your name is?"

Grasping the empty spot above my left breast, I realized I'd forgotten to put my name tag on. When Camilla put her hand on her forehead, I knew I'd drawn Mr. Dunne's attention for the infraction. Hosts and hostesses were always supposed to be wearing their name tags. "Sorry, sir. My name is Nova Blankenship. I didn't know anyone would be coming today, or I would've had my name tag on."

"Not a problem, lass." He smiled at me, and I couldn't help but smile back at him.

"Thank you, sir." Even though the man was a legend, I felt we'd get along well. "I'm excited to be working for you."

Cocking one dark brow, he asked, "Are ya now?" His Irish accent put a smile on my face that wouldn't go away.

"I am, sir." Vaguely aware that everyone was looking at us, I went on, "I was raised in this business. My parents ran a vacation resort on the Florida coast—I was put to work catering to the guests as soon as I could walk and talk. It's in my blood."

"So doing things for our guests will be like second nature to ya then," he said, putting his hand on my shoulder. "I don't know who Mrs. Chambers has assigned you to, but I want you to take care of my good friend, Mr. Christakos. He'll be here in the morning. He designed the many swimming pools and waterscapes around the island."

My breath caught in excitement. I'd admired the pools and outdoor design; to me, they should be considered works of art. "That would be my great privilege, sir. His work was the first thing I noticed when I got here—and I've been captivated ever since. Making sure he has a great time at Paradise would be an honor."

He patted my shoulder. "Good. I'm glad to make you so happy, lass. I'm sure you'll show him a wonderful time this summer."

"Oh, I will. You don't have to worry about that." I turned to find Camilla with a paper in her hand.

"Here you go. These are the notes on Astor Christakos and the things he enjoys doing. You can use these notes to make an itinerary for him. I did have you hosting someone else, but I can make this change easily enough." Camilla leaned in to whisper. "Watch yourself when you meet him. He's just about the most handsome man I've ever seen. But his demeanor takes some getting used to."

"I'll keep that in mind, thank you." I folded the paper, putting it into the pocket of my shorts.

Mr. Dunne made sure to greet each host, making conversation with each of us before excusing himself to go to his bungalow to freshen up for lunch. He told us that he looked forward to meeting the rest of the staff before the summer holiday got started. I found him to be much more down to Earth than I thought a man of his stature would be.

One of the other hostesses, Alexis, came to me with a grin on her face. "You know, I'm from Greece, too, just like Mr. Christakos. He's got a reputation as a man who works harder than most. I suppose that's how he came to be a billionaire. He came to the hotel I worked in once in Athens—for a meeting, I think. He was abrupt and almost rude, so try not to let him hurt your feelings. I just wanted to give you a head's up."

"I've dealt with tons of guests that are hard to deal with at my other jobs." I wasn't a rookie after all. "But I'll keep my emotions in check where he's concerned and try not to let him rattle me. Thank you for your advice, Alexis."

"You're welcome." She smiled at me as she told me who she would be hosting. "I've got the Chesterfields to take care of this summer. They're a married couple and they're bringing their two kids. Teenage boys." She rolled her eyes. "I'm hoping they're the quiet kind, and not the kind who'll follow me around all day trying to flirt."

"Teenage boys are the worst," I agreed. "Hopefully, their parents will rein them in for you."

"Hopefully," she said and then left me as Camilla pulled her to the side to talk to her.

I went to the restaurant we'd be eating lunch in to see if they needed any help getting things ready. I wanted to get to know every-thing I could about how things worked on the island. The place had blown me away and went beyond my expectations, and I'd had big ones. To work there forever? It would be a dream.

This place was my future, and no matter who or what tried to get in my way, I'd plow through them if I had to. Of all the vacation spots I'd worked at in my life, none were as beautiful or as full of such great people as Paradise.

As great as I thought it all was, though, I'd yet to meet the guests who would frequent the resort. I'd dealt with regular people and celebrities, but I had never dealt with the ultra-wealthy.

Mr. Dunne seemed nice enough, but would Mr. Christakos be as nice?

The day went by fast as we got everything ready for the guests. When I finally turned in, I fell into an exhausted sleep, my mind and body worn out by the busy day.

When my alarm rang bright and early, I pulled myself out of bed to shower and be ready to meet my guest.

Time to start working for real now.

All the staff lived in a building toward the back of the property, which had nicely sized rooms and suites. A communal kitchen and living space made up the front of the building, and I walked out the double doors just in time to hear a boat approaching the dock. With no time to waste, I hurried to make it there before the first guest stepped onshore.

The other hosts were gathered on the dock, standing in line, hands clasped in front of them. We all wore the same uniform: khaki shorts, a white button-down short-sleeve shirt, and sandals. The women had their hair pulled into buns that rested on the backs of their necks, and the men were all clean-shaven. Pride in how we all presented ourselves ran through me as I took my place at the end of the line.

Mr. Dunne wanted to greet his guests personally, so he stood at the front of the line. Welcoming the first to arrive with a wide grin, he said, "Good mornin,' Grant. This must be your lovely wife, Isabel." He shook the man's hand as he got off the boat, then clapped him solidly on the back before taking the woman's hand, helping her out of the boat, and placing a kiss on the top of it. "Lovely to meet you, Isabel."

"I've heard so much about you, Mr. Dunne," Isabel said with a smile. "My husband couldn't stop talking about this private club you built here for your guests to enjoy. Personally, I can't wait to see it."

Winking at her, Mr. Dunne put her hand, which he still held, into that of her husband's. "Have Grant show it off to you after you two get settled into your private bungalow." He nodded at Mrs. Chambers. "Can you see them to their personal host?"

"I can." She shook both their hands as she led them to Kyle. "This is Kyle, and he'll be your host for the summer. I gave him your information, and he's planned things out for you both. But if there are any adjustments you'd like to make, just let him know, and he'll make them for you."

Grant put his arm around his wife's shoulders, kissing the side of her head. "Thank you, Mrs. Chambers." He smiled at her with a grin I could only call wicked. "Will Mr. Chambers be joining us here?"

"Off and on," Mrs. Chambers told him. "He's got things to do as always. But when he does visit, I'll be sure to send him your way. I'm sure he'll love seeing you."

"I bet he will," Grant said. "I've got some things to teach him. I think you'll enjoy that, too."

A blush covered Mrs. Chambers's cheeks, and I wondered what that was all about. I didn't have much time to wonder before another boat came toward the dock, replacing the first boat as it pulled away to park in the marina nearby.

When Mr. Dunne turned to look at me, I knew it had to be Mr. Christakos. "Come here, Miss Blankenship."

I made my way to my boss and whispered as I approached him. "Mr. Dunne, you can call me Nova if you'd like."

"I know." He winked at me.

Feeling a little embarrassed, I plastered a smile on my face and got ready to meet the man I would be spending so much time with over the next few months. The boat pulled up, and the porter grabbed the rope that the first mate tossed to him, securing it so the guest could step easily onto the dock.

Coming up out of the cabin, I saw a man with dark brown hair that hung in thick waves to the top of the collar of his pale green button-down. The long sleeves were rolled up a quarter of the way, showing off solid, tanned forearms. Black shorts hugged his muscular butt and thick thighs. I gulped as I took in his gorgeous, olive-skinned physique.

This isn't going to be easy.

Pulling his dark Cartier, aviator-style sunglasses down his nose a bit, he looked at me. Sea-green eyes scanned my body from head to toe before he pushed the glasses back up his nose. "Galen," he greeted my boss.

Mr. Dunne reached out, shaking his friend's hand and helping him step off the boat onto the dock. "Astor. I'd like you to meet your hostess, Nova Blankenship." My boss turned his head to wink at me once more. "She prefers being called by her first name. And what should she call you?"

"Mr. Christakos." The man walked passed me, his broad shoulders swaying with his natural swagger. "Come, Nova."

Looking at Mr. Dunne, I didn't know how to react to the rude command and lack of greeting. He merely nodded at me. "Show him to his bungalow, Miss Blankenship."

I hurried to catch up to Mr. Christakos, walking by his side. "I hope your trip here was enjoyable, Mr. Christakos."

He didn't even bother to reply to my comment. Instead, he said, "I'll need you to make sure there's plenty of bottled water in my bungalow. My assistant forgot to include that on the list of things I'll need when she spoke with Camilla."

"Of course, sir. I'll arrange for a case once I've made sure you're settled into your bungalow." Stilted by his lack of warmth, I thought maybe telling him how much I loved the pools and waterscapes would help put him at ease. "Mr. Dunne told me that you designed the pools and waterscapes on the island—"

I didn't get to say another word as he came to a complete stop and turned abruptly to me, pulling his sunglasses to the end of his nose, more than a bit of aggravation showing in those gorgeous eyes this time. "I detest small talk."

Biting my tongue so as not to anger my guest and possibly lose my job, I nodded. I suddenly knew I'd be doing a lot more of that while in the presence of this man that I had to cater to all summer long.

This might not be the dream job I thought it was.

4

ASTOR

The entrancing nest of blonde bun that hung at the back of her long neck told me that my hostess had long, thick hair. I could've bet it went all the way down to her tight little ass —an ass that had instantly demanded my attention. Round and sloping into the tops of her slender thighs, it curved at the base of her spine, making a deep spot where my hand would fit perfectly.

"I detest small talk," I told her before sliding my sunglasses back up my nose and proceeding to my bungalow. She needed to know the basics about me, so I began telling her what I needed. "I get up at four every morning to work out. After I shower, I expect breakfast to be on the table."

"How long does your workout take, sir?" Nova asked me as she stayed right by my side, walking at the fast pace I'd set.

"An hour." I looked at the row of overwater bungalows we stopped in front of. "Is one of these mine?"

"Yes, sir." She pointed to the second one in. "That one is yours for the summer."

With the water being so clear, it made it difficult to tell the depth. "And how deep is the water off the deck of the bungalow?"

"Three feet." She reached into her pocket, taking out the card to unlock the door. "About six feet out, the water gets much deeper, about fifteen feet or so."

"That will make for an excellent swim. Put that on my schedule and push breakfast back thirty minutes. I'll be taking a swim after my workout, then showering." Already I'd begun making changes in my normal routine—just what I'd been hoping to do during this vacation. A certain amount of pride in myself almost made me smile.

Almost.

Nova held out her arm, gesturing for me to go inside first. "And here we are. Please allow me to show you around your home for the summer."

Stepping inside, I found myself in a hallway and walked ahead. "How many bedrooms does this place have?"

"Only the one. And one bath. The living area and kitchen are open-concept, and the high, vaulted ceiling allows for a great breeze." She stepped around me as I stopped in the living area. Shutters covered the entire wall of floor-to-ceiling windows and glass doors that looked out at the ocean. She picked up a remote and handed it to me. "This controls all the shutters, the inside temperature, and the television. The remote is well-marked, so you can see what button does what."

I pushed the button to lift the shutters, and a gorgeous scene unfolded in front of me: a large deck held an infinity pool and two lounge chairs, along with a small table for two. "Why are there two chairs?"

"In case you want to have a guest over, sir." She looked away from me, turning to the kitchen. "I've had the refrigerator stocked for you with your preferred foods. And I'll get another case of water for you in just a few minutes." She walked toward the double glass doors that led to the deck, pushing them open before looking back at me. "Care to come with me, sir? I'd like to show you how the hot tub works."

I followed her out, taking note of how her hazel eyes sparkled when her pink lips pulled into a smile. Her lower lip was plump, and the upper lip had the most perfect Cupid's bow I'd ever seen. Her teeth, white and straight, told me she took great care of herself, something I always look for in a person.

At approximately five-feet-five inches, I could tell she also exercised to keep her body in top form. Her tits, perky and large, would look amazing in a bikini top. Picturing her in a black string bikini, her blonde hair blowing in the sea breeze, gave me an instant hard-on, so I took advantage of one of the lounge chairs to hide that fact, standing behind it. "So, that's the control pad over there for the hot tub?" I asked as if I didn't already know.

"Yes, it is." She pointed at the obvious switch to turn on the jets. "All you've got to do is flip this up, and you've got action in your hot tub." Even beneath her tanned skin, I saw a pink flush fill her cheeks. "I don't know why I said it that way." She looked at the floor for a second before lifting her head. "Anyway, if you'll come with me, I'll show you to your bedroom and the adjoining bath."

"I can do that myself." The erection showed no signs of going away any time soon. And as Nova rested her hands on her hips, shifting her weight to her left foot, the sexy pose only made my boner more persistent. "Get me a water."

At first, she just looked at me, startled. "The extra case or a bottle of water?" she asked after a moment had passed.

"A bottle." I looked out at the small waves that rolled in over the clear blue water to get my mind off the distractingly beautiful woman.

Galen had to have had a hand in picking her as my hostess, the prick!

Despite his efforts, I had no plans to make any connections with any women on my vacation. Why mess up a relaxing time by adding a woman to the equation?

Nova came back with a bottle of water in one hand. She unscrewed the top, then held it out to me. "Here you go, Mr. Christakos."

Our fingertips barely touched as I took the bottle from her, making my dick just a bit harder. "You can go get that case of water now."

"Yes, sir." Nova turned to leave, and I watched her go. The way her ass moved with each step she took had me biting my lip.

Fuck, she's hot!

I moved from behind the chair to go inside. I needed to cool down—way down. "Okay, so what if she's hot?" I took a seat on the sofa and looked at the tent in my shorts.

I heard the door open and quickly grabbed a throw pillow, covering my arousal.

"Here you go, Mr. Christakos." Nova put the case of water on the counter, then opened it to put the bottles away in the fridge. "Would you like me to tell you about what kinds of activities are available to you on the island? Or are you hungry? Or..."

"No. I'll tell you my needs and wants. When I want to do something and can't figure out how to do it myself, I'll ask you about it. I don't want to be led." I put the bottle of water on the table in front of me. "Come. Let me tell you how this vacation is going to go, Nova."

Dutifully, she came to stand near me, giving me her full attention. "Of course, sir."

I liked her demeanor. Most women would've told me off or simply walked away by now—employee or no—but Nova had stayed around. That further excited me. It made me think that maybe she'd like the things I had to offer.

Or maybe she wouldn't. I knew I had to keep it professional with her before I let my mind wander too far. "I expect you to do as I say when I say it. Do you understand, Nova?"

For only a split second, her pretty eyes narrowed before she took hold of her reaction and nodded. "Yes, sir."

"Good." I leaned back. "So, let me start from where I left off. After breakfast, I'll do a bit of work on the computer. After two or three hours of work, I'll make an hour for some recreational activity. Then you may serve me lunch. I like lean meats and fresh vegetables for all of my meals. I don't like to deviate from my diet. You should already have that in the information about me."

"I do." She walked to the kitchen, opening the door to the refrigerator. "I've had suitable foods stocked in the kitchen. No carbs. No sugars. No alcohol."

"It's good to see that you can follow simple instructions." I watched her hand go to her hip and looked up to find her lips held tightly in a straight line. She wanted to respond but wouldn't allow herself to say a word. I liked that about her, too. "After lunch, I'll do a couple more hours of work, then take a break for some casual activities like strolling the beach or something. I want dinner to be served at eight sharp. After dinner, I won't need you to do anything else for me. I'll expect you to leave me alone."

Turning away from me, she said in a pleasant tone, "Have you had your breakfast already, sir?"

"I have. Today, at least the first part of it, you don't need to worry about my normal routine. I expect you to have my dinner ready at eight, and that's all I'll need from you today. I'm going to get my laptop and get to work as soon as my things are delivered."

Nova opened one of the drawers in the kitchen and then walked over to place a folder on the coffee table in front of me. "This is the itinerary I've arranged for you. It's filled with snorkeling trips, dolphin cruises, and dining in our resort's restaurants for starters. I think you should look through this and see if you might like to follow this plan. It's quite a bit better than the plan you've just laid out for yourself. What you've just described sounds an awful lot like your normal daily routine. This is a vacation, and they're supposed to be a time when you let go and give yourself and your mind a much-needed break from the routine."

I narrowed my eyes, not liking the fact that she was challenging my schedule. "I shouldn't have to explain myself to you, but I will, and I'll do it only once. I don't like to eat in restaurants alone. I love working. And I don't need anyone telling me what my vacation should be about."

Seeming unfazed, Nova went on as she pointed at the folder. "Page two has the different massage therapies available here. Page three has a lineup of the entertainment that's been planned for our guests. And I understand that you don't need anyone to tell you what a vacation is, but it can't hurt to hear about what's available to you here in Paradise, Mr. Christakos."

She smiled brightly, then turned to leave. "Maybe no one has ever offered you this advice, but I will. Relax, enjoy, and let us spoil you here. I'll be back in thirty minutes to take you to lunch at The Royal —our best chef creates masterpieces in that restaurant. I'll get myself changed and accompany you so you won't be eating alone. I am your hostess, Mr. Christakos. That means I would love to join you in any activity that you decide to take part. I'm at your beck and call, sir."

My mouth hung ajar as she walked away from me, leaving me speechless.

What the hell just happened here?

5

NOVA

After changing into a pastel-pink, boho-chic, ankle-length dress, I knocked on the door to Mr. Christakos's bungalow. "Hello, Mr. Christakos. It's me, Nova. I'm here to take you to lunch."

He opened the door wearing a linen suit and looking even more handsome than he had before. "Your little folder informed me of the dress code at The Royal. You forgot to tell me what I should wear, Nova."

Extending my arm, I said, "Ah, but I left all that information for you to read, sir. Please, let's be on our way."

He looked at my arm for a moment before shaking his head. "I don't do touching."

Dropping my arm, I smiled at him anyway and tried not to let his words bother me. "I understand."

Stepping back so he could exit the bungalow, I took a deep, silent breath, trying to relax. The man's tension seemed to be contagious.

"Small talk and touching—two things I don't do." He walked in front of me as if he knew where we were going.

When he turned left instead of right, I had to intervene. "Perhaps you would like me to lead the way? If we go in that direction, it'll be dinner time before we get to The Royal, sir."

Stopping abruptly, he turned back to me. "So it's on this side of the island? Okay."

Stifling a laugh, I walked beside him. "Yes, it's on this side of the island. By the notes I've read on your tastes in food, I do believe you will enjoy the meals Chef Alex makes at The Royal. He's half-Greek and a quarter of his menu is Greek cuisine."

He made a snorting noise. "As if all I'll eat is Greek food. I travel all over the world. I've eaten many things you've never even heard of. I find it rather presumptuous of you to assume anything about my eating habits or favorite foods, Nova."

My eyes wanted to roll so severely, they hurt. "You do remember you filled out a survey, letting us know all your likes and dislikes? But thank you for the instruction; I'll remember not to rely on the information you provided to us."

"If I recall correctly, my assistant filled that out—and she doesn't know me all that well, outside of a work environment." A genuine smile seemed to pull the corners of his chiseled lips. "And you're welcome."

"Noted. I will refrain from assuming anything about you, sir. I can assure you it will not happen again." And I meant that, too. The man had an air about him that gave me the impression that he thought of himself as a king—or at the very least, a prince.

The smile faded as he quickened his pace. I found myself making long strides to keep up with him. I had no idea what the rush was, but I wasn't going to say a word about it.

Arriving at the restaurant, he held the door open for me, which I found surprising. "Thank you, sir." Nodding at the host, I said, "I've already reserved table six for us, Donny."

"Your table's ready; you can head over there with your guest whenever you're ready, Nova." Donny looked at Mr. Christakos. "It's a pleasure to have you as our esteemed guest, Mr. Christakos. I'm Donny, and I'm sure we'll be seeing a lot of each other over the next three months."

"We'll see," my guest said, then sped off ahead of me. "Let's sit, Nova."

Looking at Donny, I discreetly rolled my eyes before following behind my guest. I tapped him on the shoulder. "This way, sir." Once again he'd led without knowing where to go. "Our table is over here. I wanted a nice view of the ocean for you."

Stopping and slowly turning around, he looked at me as if I'd purposely tried to embarrass him. "You could point in the general direction of things, Nova."

"I could." I walked toward the table near one of the windows. "But where's the fun in that?" Standing behind my chair, I said, "Table six, sir." I took a step back, giving him a chance to do the gentlemanly thing and pull the chair out for me.

He reached over and pulled the chair out. "Take your seat."

"Thank you." I sat down and watched him walk around our table for two. His butt looked amazing in his linen slacks, accentuated by the fact that he'd shoved his hands in the pockets, making the jacket lift just the perfect amount to make me all warm inside.

God, why does he have to be so hot?

If only his attitude were less...brusque, then I would've already fallen all over myself for the man. But that personality of his didn't sit well with me at all.

Being my guest, I had to find some endearing qualities in the man who gave a whole new meaning to the word *arrogant*. As if to echo my thoughts, he said, "I hope this chef is different from most of the chefs I know."

Not understanding what he meant, I asked, "Would you care to explain that to me, sir?"

"Most chefs I've met are beyond egotistical. If you dare to ask if they could leave something off or substitute broccoli for rice, they act as if you've broken a cardinal rule." One strong hand moved to push through his thick, dark waves. "They all seem to be so thin-skinned."

As hard as it was to keep my comments to myself about his use of the word *egotistical*—so far, the man seemed to be the walking definition of the word—I somehow managed.

"I can promise you that no one will treat you rudely or unkindly here. If you really want to change something, you are free to do so. But, may I add that most of the recipes our chefs use are excellent just the way they are. Trying something new isn't only fun, but it's actually good for you: mind, body, and soul."

"Says you." He opened the menu, cutting off any chance to discuss that further. "Salmon? Shrimp? Pasta?"

"Perhaps if you look at the left side of the menu you will find something more to your tastes, sir," I took the liberty to reach across the table and point to the many beef selections on his menu. "This chef prepares steaks to perfection."

"I'm a bit of a perfectionist when it comes to steak." He said, moving his gaze to the left side of the menu.

"Of course, you are," I mumbled.

I hadn't meant to say that, and when his menu slowly dropped, his green eyes piercing me, I felt a chill so strong it was as if winter had just blown in. "What does that mean, Nova?"

Knowing I'd made a terrible mistake, I quickly tried to avoid the impending catastrophe. "It means that I believe you are well-educated on proteins, beef being one of the main ones. And I believe you do know how you like your steak made. In short, I believe you are a perfectionist when it comes to steaks, sir."

My insides quivered as I waited for his reaction. The man had me on pins and needles. I couldn't recall anyone having such an effect on me. "I meant it in a complimentary way. I hope you didn't take it otherwise."

"Maybe I did." He picked up the menu, looking at it again, and I thanked God silently that he believed my very unbelievable explanation.

Perhaps so many people had placated him in the past that he thought it was a typical human reaction. Whatever it was, I made a strong mental note to watch what came out of my mouth.

It was only the first day—I couldn't let my patience slip already. I was better than that.

Petra came to wait on us, a smile on her face as she eyed my guest from behind. Winking at me, she nodded, then came up to the side of the table. "Hello, Nova. Care to introduce me to your guest?"

"Mr. Christakos, this is Petra," I said as I subtly shook my head at her. *No.* He wasn't a man to be played with—in short, he wasn't her usual fare.

Not taking my hint, she took one step closer to him. She stopped midstep when he looked sharply at her. "What are you doing?"

Her dark eyes went wide. "Um, nothing. I'm from Greece, too. Well, I was born there. My family moved..."

"Did I ask you for your life history?" he asked her.

I put my hand on my forehead, trying my best not to get mad at him for the way he'd spoken to her. "She's just being welcoming, sir." I looked at Petra. "Best to keep it professional," I said in low tones.

With a nod, she now knew what I meant when I'd shaken my head. "What can I get you to drink, Mr. Christakos?"

"Water. Half a lemon. No ice," he said, then pointed at the menu. "I want this, but not that sauce. And I want the steak prepared to one-hundred-thirty-three degrees. I want it flame-grilled with the marks prevalent on both sides." He looked at her, noticing that she hadn't written down a thing. "And your notepad is where?"

"Pardon?" Petra looked at me with panic. "I'm so sorry."

"It's okay," I tried to save the girl from further terrorization. "Just take out your notepad and write down what he's asked for." I replayed his words for her, "No sauce, flame-grilled to one-hundred-thirty-three degrees, with grill marks on both sides of the steak, Petra." I turned my attention back to my guest. "Will you be having a vegetable with that, sir?"

The way he gazed at me told me I had surprised him. "You tell her what to bring me, Nova."

I couldn't be sure if this was a test or not, but I knew one thing—I had to pick a vegetable for the man, and I'd better make the right decision. "Broccoli," I told her, then cut my eyes to his. "Steamed. No butter or salt. And not overly steamed either." He held up three fingers, and I added. "Steam it for three minutes." He nodded and smiled, and I smiled back at him. "Anything else, sir?"

Petra stopped writing to look at me after Mr. Christakos shook his head. "And you, Nova?"

"I'll have exactly the same thing as my guest. Thank you, Petra." I placed the menu on the table.

"Even the water?" she asked.

"Yes, the exact same thing." I looked at Mr. Christakos as he handed her the menus.

After she took them and left, he leaned forward, almost whispering, "Why'd you do that?"

"Order what you're having?" I asked.

He nodded. "Yes. Why did you do that?"

"I want to try things your way." I hoped to gain some footing with the man. "I like to try new things, switch things up. Life's all about doing what you've never done before—in my opinion, anyway."

"No one's ever treated me quite the way you are doing today." His green eyes danced as he looked into mine. "Are you only being this way to keep your job, Nova? And don't lie to me, because I'll know."

Reaching deep down, I tried to put my dislike for his blunt manner to the side and be honest with the man. "I'm not acting any way to keep my job. I want to know you, sir. I want to see life through your eyes for a little while. It's something I find pleasure in, seeing the world through different perspectives—it's part of why I love this kind of job."

His eyes never left mine. "That's quite remarkable, Nova?"

All I could do was smile back at him, glad to see his first true smile pulling at his lips. "I like your smile, Mr. Christakos. I look forward to trying to force it out of you as often as I can during your stay here."

And the craziest thing about that day was that I meant every last word.

6

ASTOR

The sound of waves and the ocean breeze had lulled me into a deep sleep at the end of my first day in Paradise. They continued to lull me to sleep for the next couple of weeks— I couldn't remember the last time I'd felt so well-rested.

On the fifteenth day of my vacation, Nova and I had had lunch out at one of the many restaurants on the island, but for the evening, I decided to have dinner in. She'd made me scrambled eggs and bacon per my request. After cleaning the kitchen, she'd left me for the night, just as she'd done every night thus far.

For the last ten or so years, I'd spent most of my personal time alone, preferring it that way. Nova's near-constant presence was odd, but pleasantly so. She moved about quietly and unobtrusively most of the time.

She was surprisingly determined, and her tricks were surprisingly effective on me. When she wanted me to do something, she gently and subtly urged me on until she got her way. For instance, we took a walk on the beach around dusk to catch the last bit of sunset the night before, before she'd cleaned up the kitchen and left.

Walking side by side, barefoot, I felt at peace for the first time in a very long time. There wasn't a single thought in my mind. Well... I did think about the beautiful woman at my side, about reaching out to take her hand. But I didn't act on it.

I'd had a few fantasies about Nova over the past couple weeks. Nova tied to the bed, nearly naked, her breasts rising and falling as her excitement and arousal grew. I'd woken up this morning with a hard-on that wouldn't go away. And it wasn't just my cock that wanted the woman, but my mind had begun to get in on wanting her, too.

But what I wanted to do with her—to her—wasn't something you did without prior approval. Nova had a sweetness about her that made me think I could never have her the way I wanted her, yet it only made me want her more. Almost innocent, she gave off the vibe of a woman who hadn't had much sex in her life. Not virginal, but also inexperienced enough that she didn't seem to notice that I wanted her.

Shaking off my thoughts, knowing breakfast would soon be served, I got out of the shower to get dressed. I knew Nova was already in the kitchen preparing the meal—I could smell the coffee and bacon, and my mind conjured an image of her wearing only a black bikini as she cooked for me.

Of course, I knew she wouldn't be wearing that. No, Nova came each morning dressed in her uniform of khaki shorts, sandals, and a white button-down shirt. Her blonde hair never fell out of the bun she wore—but God, how I wanted to see it all tumbling around her shoulders.

My thoughts still focused on her, I put on shorts and a T-shirt, deciding that I had to make a move. I couldn't keep going through our days like this without at least trying. My moves weren't like everyone else's—like everything else in my life, I took the abrupt approach to propositioning a woman. I didn't flirt, nor did I mean to flirt with Nova when I told her about myself—my sexual self.

Leaving my hair damp, I shook it out to let it hang in loose waves. I hadn't shaved in two days and a dark, shadowy beard had begun to grow. I wanted to look rugged, to put a picture in Nova's mind that would entice her to agree to what I wanted from her.

My patience had run out. The time had come to put my cards on the table.

Heading into the kitchen, I greeted Nova the way I did each morning. "Hello, Nova."

"Good morning, Mr. Christakos. I hope you slept well," she said as she smiled at me. "I wanted to tell you how much I enjoyed our walk on the beach last night. It was so relaxing I fell right to sleep when I got to my room."

Taking my seat at the table, I couldn't help but smile as Nova placed a steaming hot cup of black coffee in front of me. "Thank you, Nova."

My gratitude, something I hadn't expressed before, took her by surprise. Her lips parted as she looked at me with a stunned expression. "You're quite welcome, sir." She walked back around the bar to the kitchen. "Will you be taking your eggs the usual way this morning?"

"No." The time had come to change things up. "I would like some shredded cheddar cheese on top of the scrambled eggs, and some sliced tomatoes, please."

I didn't often use the word *please* either, and her reaction to that was written all over her pretty face. "Of course, sir." She moved to the refrigerator, looking over her shoulder at me. "You're in a pleasant mood this morning. Would you like to go snorkeling this afternoon?"

Snorkeling wasn't what I wanted at all. "No."

Nova went back to the bar with a ripe, red tomato in her hand. She placed it on a cutting board, then sliced it up. "Perhaps dolphin watching then?"

"No." I sipped my coffee and added. "I would like to talk to you today, Nova. And please, call me Astor."

The sound of the knife hitting the granite countertop had me looking at her, and I saw that her mouth was slightly ajar. "Of course."

"Make yourself something to eat, too. I would very much like you to join me for breakfast." I'd eaten that one meal alone every day so far. But sharing meals with Nova, taking walks with her, having conversations, it made me feel something I hadn't realized I was missing in my life. It made me feel *happy*.

"Of course," came her quick reply.

She had to have eaten before coming to my bungalow, but the woman never told me *no* about anything. And I had to admit that I adored that about her. Even if she was being paid to make me happy, I didn't care.

Talking about sex at the breakfast table didn't sit right with me. I waited until after she'd cleaned up after our shared breakfast, which I'd enjoyed just as much as I'd expected I would.

I'd taken a seat on one of the lounge chairs on the deck, waiting for her to finish with her work. When she came to me, I thought the time was at hand to talk to her openly. "Please take a seat, Nova." I pointed at the lounge chair, which was only a foot from mine.

Dutifully, she sat in the chair, and then lay back to match my own pose. "Yes, sir. It's a lovely morning, don't you think?" I didn't answer, and she hesitated before adding, "Astor?"

My cock jerked, hearing her say my name. "It is a nice morning, Nova." Closing my eyes, I could already picture her on the deck, balanced on her hands and knees, waiting for me to ram my hard cock into her soft recesses.

"So, what did you want to talk to me about?" she asked.

I turned my head to look at her. Her hands were clasped together, lying on her flat stomach—it made me ache in a way I hadn't experienced before. "You do something to me, Nova."

She turned her head to look at me with a stunned expression on her face. "What does that mean, exactly?"

I couldn't fault her for asking such a thing. I hadn't been an open book with her. I didn't know how to be an open book. But the time had come for me to open up just a bit. "I've been thinking about you. Thinking how nice it would be for you to serve me."

"I serve you now," she said with an innocent smile on her pink lips. "What more would you like me to do for you?"

"First, I would like to ask you how many sexual partners you've had in your life." I wanted to gauge her experience before getting too far ahead of myself.

The way she turned her head to look up at the sky instead of at me told me she wasn't comfortable about this line of conversation. But finally, she said, "Four."

Relieved that she'd answered me, I asked another question. "Have all of your lovers been men?"

"I haven't dipped in the lady pond, if that's what you want to know, Astor." She laughed a little, as if it was funny that I'd even ask such a thing.

I didn't always get other people's humor, and this was no exception. "Why is that funny to you, Nova?"

Sitting up, she turned in her chair to face me, putting her feet on the floor. "Because it is. I think I would like it if you got to the point."

Sitting up, I copied her pose and went for it. "I like to be in control. I like to have a woman who caters to me. I know you're being paid to be my hostess, paid to cater to me during the day. What I want from you is something you won't be paid for. I want you to submit yourself to me. And I want you to do it freely, all on your own."

The way her hazel eyes darted back and forth searching mine had me thinking she wasn't clear about what I wanted. "Are you talking about sex?"

"More than just sex, Nova. I'm talking about a relationship of sorts. Not long-term, of course."

"Of course," she said, lying back on the chair again. "Because you've got to leave at the end of July, and I've got to stay here."

Her answer made me think that she may have been thinking about me in a less than professional way, too. That got me even more excited.

"We could keep it all very simple. You will be my submissive for the rest of my vacation. When it's time for me to go, there will be no sad goodbyes. You wouldn't like me in the real world anyway. I'm much more difficult to put up with and too busy. You wouldn't get much of my time if I took you back with me, Nova."

I don't know what made me add that bit at the end—bringing

anything from this island back to the real world with me was never part of my plan.

"I don't want to go back with you anyway," she said, taking me by surprise. "My future is here. Well—I hope it's here, working at Paradise. I have no desire to go to Greece or anywhere else where there are bustling crowds and the smell of exhaust fumes in the air." She turned to me with curiosity in her eyes. "I know this might sound naïve, but I've lived most of my life in small, secluded resort towns. What does it mean to be your submissive, Astor?"

"You simply do what I want you to do. You already do a lot of it, but I want to expand that to include sex as well." I watched her chest rise as she took a deep breath then held it. She must've been doing that to steady herself. "I want to tie you up. Hold your body still so I can do with you what I want."

"And what do you want to do to me, Astor?" She bit her lower lip as lust filled her gaze.

"First, I want to run my hands all over your tight body, then smack your ass until it glows red before ramming my hard cock into your soaked pussy." My cock went hard as a rock as my heart began to pound. "I want to take you like that anywhere I choose. I don't want to ask for your permission; I want you to give yourself to me willingly, without me having to ask you a thing. If I snap, I want you to fall to your hands and knees, present yourself to me so I can fuck you hard and raw until you can't walk."

Her brows rose, and her eyes were comically huge, even though the lust remained. She'd never been talked to that way before; I could tell that by her expression—a mixture of anger and wonder at the same time. "And what do I get out of this arrangement?"

I had to laugh. I couldn't believe she had to ask. "Unending pleasure. Unimaginable orgasms. A sexual education you can take with you through the rest of your life—just to name a few of the benefits to submitting yourself to my tutelage."

"So, you want me to keep doing what I've been doing, but add in sex any time you want it?" She narrowed her eyes at me, her arms crossing against her chest in a defensive motion. "You want me to be your plaything? Some kind of sex slave?"

I hadn't counted on angering her, but knew I'd done just that. "I want to show you how much I can pleasure you by making you mine. And only for the summer, Nova. Not forever. I can make you feel things you've never felt before. There's only a fine line that separates pain and pleasure. I'd like to show you that."

"All while controlling me," she said as she glared at me. "Mr. Christakos, I am not a woman who seeks to be tamed. I am not a woman who wants anyone to control me. I do what I do for you out of the desire to do so. Yes, I get paid, but I'm in this business for the pure pleasure of seeing others have a good time.

I am not for sale or rent. Not for your sexual pleasure or anyone else's. I won't say a word about what you've asked me, and I expect you to never say a word about it either. And never bring this up to me again."

Well shit. That's not what I was expecting.

7

NOVA

I 'd never walked so fast in my life as I headed out of Astor's bungalow. His proposition had me feeling like my head would explode. I'd never been so mad before.

Kicking the sand, I shouted to no one at all, "How could he?"

I'd never presented myself as any kind of sexual being to the man. I'd never flaunted my body, never flirted with him. So how had the idea to ask me to be his submissive popped up in his head? And why did he want me that way anyway?

I could understand if he wanted a normal sexual relationship with me. I'd caught him eyeing me on more than a few occasions, and I knew he liked what he saw. And I knew he liked me. At least, he liked me more than he seemed to like anyone else I'd seen him interact with.

And I couldn't say it was one-sided. Astor's body was a thing of true beauty, and it made my body heat up in ways it never had before. And while we'd figured out a way to rub along together, his personality could be hard to take at times. His rude behavior didn't sit right with me. I knew it wasn't my job to smooth out the man's rough edges, but I had gently tried to do so anyway.

I'd thought he might be coming around after seeing the way he'd acted at breakfast that morning. He'd said *please* and *thank you* for once, finally acting like a rational human being. But never in a million years did I expect him to speak to me about those things he'd brought up today.

Once I got back to my room, I took out my laptop and did a search for what a submissive does, what would be expected of her. I found it extremely bothersome that he thought I would be into that mess.

"Tie me up? Spank me until my ass is red?" I shouted.

A knock came to my door. "Nova, are you okay in there?"

Carrie lived in the room next to mine, and I had no idea she'd be in there. "I'm fine, Carrie. Thank you for asking."

"Do you want to talk?" she asked through the door.

"No, thank you." I knew I couldn't vent to anyone about what had made me so angry. "I'm fine. Really, I am."

"Okay, then. If you say so." I heard her footsteps as she walked away.

I had to get myself under control. I had to stop talking—or shouting—to myself before I alerted everyone to my distress. But the fact remained that I'd never been so pissed.

How can he think I would go for that? What kind of woman does he think I am?

One picture on my computer screen showed a woman on her knees, holding up a cup of tea or coffee or something as a man stood over her, running his hand over her cheek as she looked up at him.

"Disgusting!"

Another knock came to my door. "Nova?"

Now Donny had overheard me. "Sorry. Just saw something yucky on my computer. I'll be quiet."

"Okay," he said, then left.

Staff housing wasn't anywhere near as private as guest housing. I would have to shut my mouth, or everyone would end up thinking I was crazy.

As I sat there, looking at picture after picture, I began to feel sick to my stomach at the thought of how the rest of the summer would play. I couldn't bear the thought of not only having to see Astor for lunch, but having to see him every day and act like I was on good terms with him.

How on Earth can I do that now, knowing what he wants to do with me?

If I went to Camilla to ask her to switch me to another guest, she'd ask why I wanted that. I couldn't do that. I felt a sense of loyalty toward Astor, and I didn't want his business to be gossiped about. Why I still felt loyal to him didn't make a hell of a lot of sense to me right now, but that's just the way it was.

Maybe it was because he liked me, even when he clearly didn't like anyone else. I didn't know. I did know one thing though, I had to make sure he understood that I couldn't be what he wanted me to be. That is, if he didn't already realize that after I'd given him my answer that morning—which I hoped he had.

Lunch would be coming up in only a few hours. I had already planned to cook for him in his bungalow as he'd asked me the day before. Now I wondered if he'd made those plans with other thoughts in mind—thoughts about what he wanted me to do, what he wanted to do with my body.

"Sick!" I shouted.

"You okay, Nova?" came Julie's voice, another hostess who had a room just down the hall.

"Yes, I'm fine." I put my hand over my mouth to hold in any further outbursts.

Going back to looking at pictures of submissive women, I found that some were posed with gags in their mouths, handcuffs around their wrists, and blindfolds, too. At least I knew Astor had none of those things with him. I'd been the one to unpack for him, and I knew he didn't have the paraphernalia of a typical dominant.

Sitting on my bed, I began to wonder how many submissives had studied under the man's *tutelage*, as he'd put it. Did he have one who traveled with him? And if so, why hadn't he brought her with him to the island?

Lying back, I closed my eyes to try to relax. The image of Astor with some negligee-clad woman on all fours filled my mind. I opened my eyes, feeling even more anger.

Jealousy?

Why would I feel jealous about him even hypothetically being with another woman? Why would I care? And why did my heart beat so hard at the thought?

I needed fresh air to help settle my addled mind. Closing my laptop—I didn't want anyone to accidentally see what I'd looked up —I left my room to take a walk on the beach.

The beach on the other side of the island, so there would be no chance of running into Astor.

Coming up behind a couple who strolled hand in hand, I recognized them as Grant and Isabel, the first guests to arrive on the island. "Good morning, you two," I greeted them as I came up on one side to pass them, my pace much faster than theirs.

"Morning," Isabel said as her husband nodded at me. "How are things going with Mr. Christakos?"

"Fine," I said, far too quickly.

Grant laughed. "That good, huh?"

I felt my cheeks heat with a blush. "Well, you know. It can't always be roses, right?"

Isabel reached out to touch my arm. "We've known him for years. I know he can be a bit," she paused, "abrupt. But he's a very smart, perceptive man."

Like a key in a lock, her words made a vault open inside my head. "You've known him for years?"

Grant nodded. "He belonged to a club I had a while back."

"What kind of club?" I had to ask.

Isabel looked up at her husband as she answered me, "A secret club. It doesn't matter." Then she looked at me. "Astor gets along with you better than I've ever seen him get along with anyone."

With a huff, I said, "Yep."

"You seem agitated, Nova," Grant said. "Is everything alright?"

"Peachy," I said, then picked up my pace once more. "You two have a nice walk now. Bye."

I had a lot of steam to walk off, and strolling alongside the happy couple wasn't going to get that done for me. As I left the beach to walk through the trees, hoping the filtered sunlight would help cool me down, I found someone coming out of what seemed to be a tree trunk. "Kyle?"

Pulling on what looked like a thick brown vine, Kyle looked like a deer caught in the headlights. "Nova!"

"What the heck is this, Kyle?" I asked as I looked at the tree. I couldn't distinguish any kind of door on it at all. "I just saw your guests walking on the beach. Does this have anything to do with them?"

He took me by the hand, leading me away from the weird tree. "Don't ask. You need to forget what you've just seen."

"I didn't see much. Only you, coming out of a tree trunk." I looked over my shoulder as he tugged me along. "Kyle, really, what is that?"

"A secret," he said.

Thinking back to my conversation with Isabel and Grant, I recalled her saying something about them having a secret club. One that Astor had belonged to once. "Come on, Kyle. I need to know what that is back there. My guest used to be in a secret club with Grant and Isabel. I want to know if that place has anything to do with my guest."

"He hasn't visited that place, I can tell you that much," he told me. "And you can't bring it up, anyway. Things of that nature might upset outsiders."

"Outsiders? Outside of what, exactly?" I asked.

He laughed as he hurried me along. "If you're on the outside, you'll never know, Nova. Don't worry about it. It's out of your league anyway."

"Out of *my* league?" I asked, feeling a little insulted, even though I had no idea what he was talking about. "But it's in *your* league?"

"Yep." His hand gripped mine tighter. "It's the reason I got this gig here on the island. And I've signed a non-disclosure agreement, making it impossible for me to tell you more than I already have. And you can't tell anyone about what you saw me doing either." He stopped just before we left the cover of the trees. Pressing my back to one of them, he looked me right in the eyes. "I mean it, Nova. You can't tell a soul about what you've seen. It's only for a select number of guests, so just forget about it. Promise me." He took me by the shoulders, holding me tight. "Say it."

"But..."

"Say it," he demanded. "Promise me you won't tell a single soul about what you've seen."

"But why?" I asked, feeling curious about what all the secrecy was about.

"Because it will get you fired if you say something to the wrong person. I don't want that to happen to you." He pushed me even harder against the tree. "Now promise me."

"You're hurting me, Kyle," I told him. "I promise I won't say a word. Now let me go."

His hands came off me, and a smile returned to his face. "Cool. I'm serious about you getting fired. Of course, if your guest takes you to that place, then you'll know why it's such a huge secret. He might want to, since he was once in a club with my guests."

"You know what kind of club they had, don't you?" I walked next to him as we made our way back to the staff housing building.

"Yep." Kyle winked at me. "To be honest, Nova, I don't think your guest will ask you to go with him, even if he does go. I doubt you're into the kind of lifestyle he's into."

And just like that, I knew what Kyle was trying so hard to keep me from knowing. He was a part of some nasty little sex club.

And right here on the island!

8

ASTOR

Obviously, I'd gone about my proposition to Nova the wrong way. I'd never asked a vanilla to give the lifestyle a try before. All of my submissives came from a club I'd belonged to once. But the club had been destroyed, and the owners never saw fit to open a new one. I'd never even looked for another club to join after that, having gotten too caught up with my business by that point.

My usual forthright way hadn't worked for me this time, and I had to figure out how to smooth things over with Nova. We did have the whole summer to deal with, after all.

I didn't want her asking to switch with another hostess, something I worried she might be considering. I hoped she would come to my bungalow for lunch as we'd planned. Worrying about whether someone was mad at me was a new experience for me—it wasn't normally something I cared much about. But having Nova mad at me bothered me immensely.

I'd been sitting on the deck when I heard the front door close. Nova didn't call out a greeting to me the way she usually did, but I knew it must be her. I got up from my chair to go inside.

Her back was to me as she busily put things into the cabinet. "I'm sorry, Nova," I said.

"Good," she snipped.

My hands balled into fists, her tone not sitting well with me. "No reason to be snippy."

She spun around, her eyes narrowed, and took a deep breath as her eyes closed. "Okay. I accept your apology, Mr. Christakos."

"Astor," I reminded her. "I want you to call me by my first name from now on. No more Mr. Christakos."

"Fine," she said, then went to get the meat from the fridge. "If you want anything, you need to ask me for it from now on. I've been thinking about the way I've been treating you—catering to you at all hours of the day. I think that must be the reason why you thought I would accept your proposal. I'll stop being so—for lack of a better word—*submissive* to you. Maybe that will change the way you think of me, Astor." She looked right into my eyes. "I took the liberty of looking up what it means to be a submissive, and I don't like any of it."

"Okay," I said as I sat down on the other side of the bar. "Tell me what you've found out about it, and maybe I can help you understand it better."

She huffed as she put a whole chicken on a cutting board. "I found out that men like you want a woman groveling at your feet." The meat cleaver she held slammed through the backbone of the raw chicken as she split it in two.

"I don't like groveling," I let her know. "That's not what that position is about—it's about showing your dominant that you're devoted to him. It shows how much you adore serving him. And the act of kneeling does more than that. It actually strengthens your core muscles—gives you better posture, too."

She looked up at me with sorrow-filled eyes. "I saw a picture of a dominant making his Sub kneel on dried beans. He only meant to hurt her, not help her with her muscles or posture."

I had to give it to the girl—she must've delved deep to find pictures like that. "There are some dominants that have an evil streak in them. I can assure you that I'm not that way."

She chopped off one of the chicken's legs as she asked, "What way are you, then, Astor?"

"I think a woman's body is the most beautiful thing that's ever been created. I think long, toned muscles make it that much more appealing." I reached over and moved one finger over the back of her hand, the one that held the large knife. "I think holding certain things back, like touch, only make it that much better when you finally do touch each other. I think keeping your lips off your Sub's body while you fuck her relentlessly makes the kiss at the end that much sweeter."

She held her breath as I moved my finger up her arm. I knew what she felt because I felt it, too: pure bliss, pure energy, pure arousal—and all that from only the touch of my fingertip.

"Astor, why do you need to be in control?" Her eyes were dark with emotion. Nova wanted more than she allowed herself to believe.

"Someone has to be in control, Nova," I let her know as I moved my hand back to rest on the countertop in front of me. I saw her eyes move to my hand and knew she already missed my touch. "Alone, not part of a couple, you take control of yourself, don't you?"

"Of course, I control myself. That's exactly why I don't understand why you would want to control me, Astor. If I let you control me, then what's left of me?" She put the knife down to really look at me, her eyes drooping a bit at the edges. "Haven't I pleased you so far? Haven't I made you happy?"

"You have," I admitted.

Her shoulders moved with a shrug. "Then why control me now? I know what you want without you needing to control me. I'm attracted to you. I know you're attracted to me. If you'd made a move, I would've accepted it. And not because I have to, either. I would've accepted it because I wanted to."

"If I told you that I wanted to look at your body as you kneel— that I would love seeing you that way—would you drop to your knees?" I asked her.

She shook her head. "Of course not. I'm not about to go dropping to my knees because you tell me to or because you snapped your fingers, either. I'm not into being broken, Astor. To me, what you want is a trained animal, not a sexual partner."

"Your strong will isn't something I want to break, Nova. That's exactly what I want to witness. I want to see you use that strong will to satisfy me. I want your desire to please me to be as strong as your will to succeed in life. When you told me about your plans to go to college, I could see that willful spirit of yours glowing in your eyes." I saw the way her eyes lit up a bit and thought she might finally be getting the idea of what it truly meant to be a submissive.

"I'll get something from going to school. What would I get out of using my will to please you?" she asked as she chopped off another of the chicken's legs with a swift blow.

I didn't like the tense atmosphere between us. While I knew she had concerns about what I wanted, I saw no reason for her to react with any kind of violence. "Nova, there's no reason for you to feel hostile toward me. I will never do a thing to you that you don't agree to. I promise you that. Now, cut the rest of the chicken up normally, not like you're a medieval butcher."

The way she leveled her eyes on me told me she might just pick that knife up and bring it down on my head. But then she placed it in the sink before washing her hands. "Talking to me as if I'm a child won't earn you any points, Astor." She dried her hands and stooped to get a glass dish out from under the sink. Walking to the cabinet, she pulled out a bottle of barbeque sauce then poured some of it into the dish before placing the chicken into it. "How many subs have you had?" She poured the rest of the sauce to cover the meat then tossed the empty bottle into the trash before washing her hands again.

"Six," I told her and watched as she shuddered. "None of them lasted very long. It's been a while since I've had one—tending to my company became more urgent than tending to any of them."

She placed clear plastic wrap over the chicken, then walked outside to turn the outdoor grill on before coming back to ask, "Did any of them last more than a couple of months?"

I took her line of questioning as a positive. "No. And all of my interactions with them were at a club I belonged to. I've never had a submissive be a part of my day-to-day life—not the way I want it to be with you."

"Like a real relationship," she said as she picked up the pan to take it outside. "Only this one would end when summer does. And I'm not supposed to get attached." She looked over her shoulder at me as she walked out. "Right?"

"Right." I followed her, thinking she might be actually be giving it a second thought. "No hard feelings, no fighting, no breaking up. Just some fun. You get to learn some new things, and we both get to have lots of hot sex."

Placing the meat on the grill, she sighed before taking the pan back inside to wash it. I could tell an internal battle raged within her. The woman was attracted to me; she'd admitted that she'd thought about us being together. That in itself had to be hard to combat. If she could just get over the submissive part, then we'd both get what we wanted.

Following her, I took my seat at the bar once again as she started preparing a salad. "I would like to be honest with you, Astor."

"I would like that, too," I said as I picked up the bottle of water she'd put on the countertop for me. "Thank you for the water, Nova."

She looked at the bottle in my hand. "Hm?" Her eyes went wide. "I hadn't even realized I'd gotten that for you. Just used to doing it, I guess."

I tried hard to hide the smile that crept over my lips. The woman knew me—even before she'd really known me, she knew me. "You're perfect."

"Not exactly." She placed the romaine lettuce in a large bowl and began to pull the leaves off and shred them by hand. "See, the thing is, I can't turn my feelings off and on the way you must think I can. Even as it is right now, I know I'm going to miss you when you leave. I'll miss your abruptness, your arrogance," She laughed, and it hurt my pride a bit that it sounded self-deprecating. "And it's only been a couple of weeks. The truth is I've never had to play host one-on-one like this before. This is kind of intense, you know?"

"I've never been around anyone other than my family for as much as I've been around you, so I know what you're saying, Nova." I stopped to think about the circumstances we'd been put into. "Maybe this attraction is just a byproduct of all the time we've spent together."

She stopped what she'd been doing to look me in the eyes. "I thought you were hot from the moment I saw you."

"Yeah, I knew that." I smiled at her, and I could tell it was a different smile than any I'd given anyone else. "I thought you were cute."

She threw a lettuce leaf at me. "Cute? Only cute?"

"It takes me longer to really look at people," I explained to her. "But by the end of lunch that first day, I had it bad for you."

She laughed as she got back to work making the salad. "And it only took you two weeks to make your move, and when you did, it was a real doozy."

I wanted to be honest with her, despite her objections. "Look, here's the deal, Nova. I don't like vanilla sex. And if you think we can walk hand-in-hand down the beach, then come back here and make love, then you're in for so much disappointment. Can you just try things my way? If you hate it, we can stop."

Placing the bowl of salad on the table, she turned to look at me. "I *will* hate it, Astor. I'll make your lunch and then leave you alone. I need to put some space between us. I can see that very clearly now."

I let out a deep breath, trying to hide my disappointment. *How do things keep going so wrong?*

9

NOVA

The next few days I did only the basics for Astor, keeping as much distance between us as I could. But no matter how much space I put between us, I couldn't stop thinking about him and what he wanted. I kept finding myself grabbing my laptop to learn more and more about the world of submissive and dominant couples.

While some articles made me feel sick, there were others that I actually found...intriguing. And I found out that I actually had many submissive traits. I figured that must be what had made Astor proposition me—he'd picked up on my naturally submissive tendencies.

At first, I felt like something must be wrong with me. Why did I have this urge to please nearly everyone? But then I thought about how my life had been since day one, and it all made sense to me. I'd grown up watching both my parents be hospitable day in, day out, and I had picked up on all of that.

Seeing what someone wanted or needed before they even asked for it was second nature to me. And Astor was my guest, not a friend or anything like that. If he'd been just a friend or guy I'd met, then I most likely wouldn't have exhibited those traits so obviously. But he wasn't a guy I'd just met, and I'd already treated him in a way that made him look at me in ways he shouldn't.

A submissive partner. How come he can't look at me as a romantic partner?

I'd never been in love. I thought I might have been a time or two, but it never lasted. If there was anything I wanted more in my life than to go to college, it was to experience real love—not just hot sex.

Not that I'd ever experienced hot sex, either. Just the regular kind. And kind of bland, too. And short.

Man, I've really got to get out more.

And here was a man who wanted to show me more. I had a man wanting to give me experiences I might never get the chance to have otherwise. Would I really pass all that up? And for what? More boring, vanilla sex that didn't involve love either?

I stared at my computer screen, looking at a picture of a woman being blindfolded as she kneeled in front of her Dom. I wondered how she felt. *Scared? Nervous? Aroused?*

Then I stopped wondering about her and closed my eyes, putting myself in her place. My hands tied behind my back. My naughty negligee split in between my legs to give my Dom access to my most intimate parts. His hands running over my shoulders as he moved the blindfold around to cover my eyes.

The darkness tantalized, sheltering me from reality. His hands moved down my arms then over my breasts, making me suck in my breath as my body trembled with a need so strong I would gladly endure any punishments if it meant I got release. All that mattered was that he made me his. As long as he sank his hard cock into me, I would suffer anything.

When I opened my eyes, I felt tears rolling down my cheeks. "Can I really give in to him?" I whispered. "Would that be a slap in the face to who I am? Or would it only add to who I am?"

He'd said we could stop if I hated it. *But what if I loved it?*

What if I didn't want him to leave me at the end of summer? What then?

Somehow I knew being with him would break me. In one way or

another, Astor Christakos would break me. I might be able to control in some way how he did it, but it would happen regardless.

Meeting that man had been fate, written in the stars long before we'd actually met. Something inside told me that. So, what was I waiting for?

It had been three hours since I'd seen him at lunch. We'd eaten at one of the restaurants instead of his bungalow. I'd told him I didn't want to be alone with him anymore, and he agreed to eat out with me.

Astor had become incredibly accommodating, and that had me thinking he might actually care about me. I wouldn't have thought him capable when I'd first met him, but here we were. And if he cared about me, then maybe he wouldn't break me. Maybe we could have more than he thought.

Or maybe I'm just fooling myself.

Getting up, I walked into the bathroom and pulled my hair out of the bun I'd put it in that morning. It fell in long waves down my back. I wanted to do something different today with Astor, so I went to put on my bathing suit. We'd never gone into the water together before, and I wanted to do that with him. I wanted to see if he could just have fun with me, really let loose for once. But I also wanted to look in his eyes when he saw my body for the first time, nearly naked.

The way Astor looked at me on a normal day made me hot. His sea-green eyes would rake over me every time he saw me. *Will they linger on my breasts when he sees me like this? My ass? My face?*

Putting on my black bikini, I tied it tightly then put on a white lace cover-up over it. Leaving off my shoes, I left my room to go to his bungalow.

My heart raced once I got to his door. With a quick knock, I called out, "Astor? Are you here?" I opened the door.

"Nova?" he asked as he sat up on the sofa.

"Were you napping? Did I wake you?" I asked as I stepped inside, closing the door behind me.

He blinked a few times and then rubbed his eyes with the back of his hand. "Yeah." He looked at me again, and a smile formed on his lips. "What do you have on?"

"I wanted to go for a swim and see if you wanted to join me." I watched his eyes as they moved over my body. "So, you wanna take a swim?"

"Sure." He got up, dropping his shorts. His black Speedo underneath told me he'd already taken a dip before I'd gotten there.

I pulled the white cover-up off and delighted in the way his eyes lit up and roamed over my body, lingering on my tits. I walked toward him, passing by him as I headed to his deck. "Is the water warm today?"

"Yeah," his voice sounded near my ear as he came up right behind me. "It's hot."

I almost laughed—his demeanor had changed to more of a lovesick puppy than the arrogant man he was most of the time. "Good. I like it when it's nice and warm."

Walking down the stairs to the water, I waded in. He came in right behind me. "I like your hair better when you have it down." He confidently ran one hand through it. "It's silky, too. I knew it would be."

Turning around to face him, I looked at his thick waves. "May I?"

"May you what?" he asked, his attention captured once more by my tits.

"Run *my* hands through *your* hair?" I laughed. "What else?"

He frowned a little. "I would rather you not do that."

With a shrug, I fell back to wet my hair, ducking under the water and coming back up to find him staring at me still. I splashed him a bit. "Stop staring!"

"You're just so...," he shook his head. "No, that's not a strong enough word. You're so..."

"Pretty?" I asked as I batted my eyelashes at him.

He shook his head. "No, that's not strong enough either. You're like a goddess. A curvaceous, tanned, gorgeous goddess."

He reached out for me, but I laughed and took a couple of steps backward. "No touching, remember?" I turned and began to swim into deeper water.

He grabbed my ankle, pulling me back. "You sure about that?" His hands slid over my wet skin then he took me in his arms, holding me tightly. I felt his erection, barely hidden by his tight swimwear. "You like my touch."

Goosebumps covered me from head to toe—but I wasn't about to tell him that. "Do I?"

He nodded. "You do." Moving one hand along my arm then up to caress my cheek, I nearly blacked out at how amazing it felt. My eyes closed as he moved his knuckles across my cheekbone. "See, you like it when I touch you, Nova."

Moving my arms, I wrapped them around his neck. "Wanna see if I like it when you kiss me?"

He didn't say a thing, just looked into my eyes, then at my lips. "I know you'll like it. And I know I won't stop if I do that right now."

I had to know what he would do to me if I let him. "And what would you do after that, Astor?"

He ran his hands up my arms, taking my hands in his own, pulling them away from his neck to secure them both behind me in only one of his big, manly hands. "I would tie your hands behind your back."

"But then I couldn't hug you." I gave him a sexy grin. "Where's the fun in that?"

He turned me around, still holding my wrists together, and pushed my body to bend forward. "Then I would bend you over like so."

He pressed his swimsuit-covered hard-on against my ass and moisture blossomed inside of me. "Not a bad move, Astor."

His hand moved from my back, running around my ribs then up to skim over my tit. He slipped his hand inside the thin material of my bikini top to take my hard nipple between his fingers. My breath caught and a new heat flushed through me.

"I would check to make sure you were getting aroused." His hand moved again, going down the outside of my thigh before moving between my legs, spreading them and palming my sex. "I would make sure you were ready to take me inside you, and I would demand you be quiet while I fucked you. Since we're outside and could be caught, the silent part would be a necessary evil, I'm afraid. If we were inside, where no one could hear your moans of pleasure, then I would let you make all the noise you wanted to."

"Ah, the controlling part. I see." I straightened up then pulled my wrists out of his grip before turning to face him. He released me easily. "I've been thinking a lot lately."

He gave me a cocky smile. "I can see that."

"I don't understand all of it. And I don't like most of it." I looked over the chiseled pecs of his wide chest and on down to the ladder that split his stomach into six pieces. "But I know I want it."

"You want *me*," he said, and it sounded as if he was correcting me. "You want *me*. You don't want *it*. I know you don't."

"I thought it was a package deal?" I asked him. Was he coming around to making some compromises?

He nodded. "If you want me, you've got to agree to what I want."

Nope, no compromising.

"And if I do?" I asked.

He laughed a little. "Then I do to you what I've just explained. And then you go inside and make me dinner—just like normal. Later, I would let you give me a bath, and I'd see what I wanted from there."

My eyes rolled all on their own. "Whoa, the first part sounded great. But then it kinda went downhill from there."

"That's what I thought you'd say. You're not ready for this. You most likely never will be." He turned away from me, climbing up the stairs and leaving me alone in the water. "You're vanilla, Nova. That's okay. This isn't for everyone." And then he walked inside.

Son of a bitch!

10

ASTOR

L ooking up at the ceiling as I showered, trying to douse the flames that Nova had ignited in my body, I tried to think of anything that would calm the arousal she'd created. "Damn woman!"

I wanted to make her mad by brushing her off, telling her she was vanilla. I wanted to give her the tiniest taste of what I could do for her, and then leave her hanging out to dry when she wouldn't give me everything I wanted.

I knew it wasn't playing fair, but I was beyond that at this point.

She'd stormed out of my bungalow after I left her alone in the water. I wanted to rush after her, an urge I've never had in my life. And that impulse annoyed me.

What did I think would happen? Did I think I could be her Dom and then leave her when summer came to an end? Never think about her again? Never want to keep things going?

Nova had no idea the hold she had on me already, and we hadn't even had sex. Maybe having her as my Sub would be a giant mistake. Maybe she would be the one to break me. I didn't know, and didn't want to find out either.

But even as these thoughts passed through my head, my mind

wandered off, thinking back to Nova. Thinking about how badly I wanted to see her kneeling on my floor, sucking my cock on demand. Falling all over herself for me—and only me. It filled me with a need I'd never known.

Maybe that's what prompted me to get out of that shower, put on some shorts—and nothing else—and go off in search of the staff's quarters. As I walked into what appeared to be a living area, I asked the first person I saw, "Where does Nova live?"

He pointed to the hallway on the right. "Third door on the left, Mr. Christakos."

"Is she in there?" I asked him before going to the room.

"She is." He smiled at me. He looked like he was about to say more, but I cut him off.

"Mind your business." I headed to the hallway and stopped in front of her door. A poster hung there with a white kitten and the words, 'Today's your day, baby,' written across the bottom.

It would be her day alright. I didn't knock; I just turned the doorknob and pushed it open, finding it unlocked. As the door opened, I caught her with her back to me and not a stitch on. "Shit!" she screeched.

I stepped inside and closed the door in a hurry. "You should've locked your door, Nova. What the hell?"

"I was kind of in a bad state of mind, Astor." She picked up a blanket off her bed then threw it around her body. "What are you doing here? And how did you know which room is mine? And what makes you think you can just barge in on me anyway?"

"I—uh, damn it, Nova, stop asking me questions." I had some questions of my own. "Why did you come to me like that today?"

She held the blanket in one hand as she threw her other hand around, gesturing in the air. "I want you. I know I'm a fool for thinking I can have you in some way that feels normal to me. But damn it, I want you! I've never had great sex. Or even good sex." She looked at the floor as her cheeks went red. "The only orgasms I've ever had, I had to give myself."

"What a shame." She'd stunned me. "Not one of those guys could do that for you?"

She shook her head. "No. Not one of them. And then you came along and—well, quite honestly, you make me wet without even trying." Looking up at me, she went on, "Is it so wrong for me to want to see what sex would be like with you, without having to commit to being your Sub?"

I knew myself well enough to know that I would treat her like one anyway. I didn't know any other way. But I thought it seemed like it was about time she got a small taste of what it meant to be my Sub.

"No, it's not wrong of you, Nova." I stepped further into her room. "Drop that blanket and get on your knees. I'll give you a sample of what it means to be mine. If you like it, you can decide whether you want more or not."

"Really?" she asked, looking like she didn't quite believe me. "No strings?"

"None." I dropped my shorts, leaving myself as naked as she was underneath that flimsy blanket. "Here, we're on even ground."

Her hands shook as she let the blanket drop. "We'll have to be quiet. These walls are paper thin."

"Works for me." I knew how to be quiet. It was Nova who I thought might have a difficult time. If she'd never experienced an orgasm at the hands of someone else, then she was about to lose her mind.

Moving in close to her, I took her hands in mine as she whispered, "Do you have any protection? Because I don't."

"We won't need it. I'm not going to penetrate you with my cock." I looked around the room and found an extension cord. "I'm just going to please you."

"You are?" she asked, her lips quivering.

Letting her go, I went to unplug the long, thin cord then came back to her. "Put your hands behind your back."

She did as I'd demanded without any hesitation. "Okay."

Wrapping the cord around her wrists, I bound them the way I'd wanted to since the moment I set eyes on her. I saw a dark blue scarf hanging from her mirror and went to get it. "I'm going to put this scarf around your eyes. You'll let yourself go a lot more easily without your sight."

"Okay," she said in a breathless whisper.

After I tied it tight over her eyes, I turned her to face the bed and bent her over it. "I'm not going to spank you tonight, Nova. It makes too much noise."

"Okay," she said again. She'd turned into such an agreeable person so quickly. I almost laughed at how much she'd changed in only a matter of days.

The hardest part would be not sticking my already aching cock inside her. But I would resist it. I had to leave her wanting more, or this might well be the only time I got to be with her this way.

I would get off, just not inside of her. Pulling her ass cheeks apart, I heard her gasp as I touched her with the tip of my cock. "I'm not going to put this in you tonight. I'm just going to use the shaft to arouse you—to drive you crazy."

I pushed her further up on the bed, laying her on her stomach before lying on top of her, putting my cock between her ass cheeks like a hot dog.

"That feels weird," she said quietly.

"No talking." I grabbed the tops of her shoulders and began moving back and forth, stroking my cock between her cheeks.

She made a soft moan as her body went limp underneath mine. Slipping one hand beneath her, I found her sex and used my fingers to manipulate her clit, and she made another soft moaning sound.

Once I had that pearl as swollen as it could get, I moved my finger down, slipping it into her tight hole. "Oh, shit. You're so tight. Fuck." Only one finger would fit.

My cock got even harder as I moved faster just thinking about how her tight pussy would fit around me like a glove. Inside, she felt hot and juicy, and I felt like I was about to start salivating.

I couldn't stop myself from having a taste. I moved off her, rolling her onto her back then yanking her ass to the end of the bed as I got on my knees. Heat came off her pussy in waves as I put my mouth on her, running my tongue through her folds as she writhed and moaned.

"You have to be quiet, baby." I kissed her intimately, running my tongue around her clit before moving lower and sticking it into her, fucking her with my tongue as her legs clamped around my head.

I had to force her legs apart so I could go in deeper. With one hand on my cock, I stroked it as I ate her until she came with a glorious gush that filled my mouth with her sweet nectar.

Her legs clamped down on me so hard as she climaxed, it took everything I had to keep her spread open. She moaned and groaned as her body let it all go. Nearly there, I stood up, pumping my cock until I came all over her tits.

Barely able to breathe, I looked at her as she lay on the bed covered in my semen, her body pink with the heat of her orgasm. "You like that?"

"Um, hm," she moaned.

I pulled up one of her legs before tossing the blanket on her chest to wipe away the cum. Grazing my lips along the inside of her thigh, I kissed my way across her stomach, wiping away my remnants and the blanket from her tits so I could kiss them.

Sucking them soft and easy, I loved the little sounds she made. Not as quiet as she should've been, but as quiet as I could expect of her on our first go. Licking one nipple as I played with the other, I moved my body to cover hers.

"If you're a good girl, I'll give you more—if you want it. But not today. I'll give you time to think about it, time to decide if you want to be in my bed and want to serve me and only me. If you decide to become my Sub, it would mean that I own your ass until I leave. No one gets to touch what's mine. Understood?"

"Yes." She arched her body up. "I'm aching for you, Astor. Can't take my answer now and give me what I'm craving?"

"You think you're ready to answer now?" I chuckled as I kissed my way up her neck. "You're still feeling the afterglow. It's not your usual state and not one where you should ever make big decisions. Hell, if I asked you to marry me, you would say yes right now, I bet. If I asked you to let me take you in the ass, you would say yes right now, too."

She moaned. "You're right."

"I'm always right, baby." I kissed her cheek, and she turned her head to catch my lips. I pulled back, out of her reach. "Bad girl," I whispered.

Then I pulled off the scarf so I could look into her pretty hazel eyes. She blinked then focused her eyes on mine. "I do feel like a bad girl. And as crazy as it sounds, my ass is quivering. It wants to feel your hand slamming down on it so badly."

She'd surprised me. "You're amazing like this, baby. I hope that when all the endorphins calm, and you go back to your regular way of thinking, you'll remember all of this."

"How can I forget?" she asked me.

I knew she probably wouldn't forget, but she might feel embarrassed. I didn't want her to. "I hope you don't." I eased down, my lips barely touching hers. "I hope you want to become mine, Nova. If you agree to be my submissive, it will mean moving you into my bungalow with me for the rest of my stay here."

Straining, she pulled her head up to make my lips mold to hers. My head went light as she opened her mouth, and against my better judgment I moved right in. Lost in her kiss, I knew I'd made a terrible mistake by kissing her so soon.

Who will own who by the time summer comes to an end?

11

NOVA

After the best kiss I'd ever had, Astor left me alone to think about becoming his Sub. He'd told me not to come to his bungalow for dinner that evening. He said he wanted me to leave him completely alone, so I could make a rational decision that would leave me with no regrets.

That night I slept better than I ever had. My body felt so relaxed that I almost felt boneless. I'd never thought of myself as particularly tense, and I'd had no idea that I could feel this serene. I'd had my fair share of massages—the perks of resort life—and even the effects of those couldn't hold a candle to the way Astor's attentions had left me. He'd taken me to new heights, and then left me feeling like jelly, wrung out from the pleasure.

When I woke to a knock on the door the next morning, I found a smile on my lips at the thought that it might be him. I grabbed a robe then went to answer the door. "Good morning." When I opened it, I found a vase of pink roses covering someone's face. "Oh!"

Laura, from the island's boutique, moved the flowers away from her face. "Someone has an admirer." She handed the crystal vase to me. "Do you even need me to tell you who sent you these, Nova?"

Shaking my head, I bit my lip. "No, I don't. Thank you, Laura. These are beautiful."

"Do we have our first love connection of the island?" She laughed as she eyed me knowingly.

"Who knows?" I took the vase of flowers, placing them on the small table in my room. "It's definitely too early to start thinking about love just yet."

"Sure it is." She turned with a wink and left me alone with my unexpected present.

I closed the door, heading to the bathroom to take a shower and get dressed for the day. There was no card with the flowers, a sign that Astor would stay true to his word. He would leave me alone to make my decision.

The thing is, I'd already made my decision.

I wanted this. I wanted to see what it would be like to give myself to that man. I didn't care what happened after that. I wanted the experience more than I'd ever wanted anything.

As I stood under the warm water of the shower, I wondered what it would feel like when he finally took me. He'd finally shown me what a real orgasm was supposed to feel like, but I knew there was more. I knew that no pleasure would compare to what would happen when he was finally inside me.

The thing that surprised me the most was how much I wanted to feel his hands on me, smacking my ass, holding me down. I shivered as I remembered how it had felt the day before.

What I'd said to Laura was the truth—love wasn't even a thought in my head at that time. No, just lust and an urgent need to feel his massive body on top of mine, gyrating and pinning me to his mattress. Or bent over in the water as he thrust his massive cock into me from behind would be just fine, too. I wanted it all, every last bit of anything he'd give me.

I realized I would enjoy our time together and then hold our summer of passion in my memories forever, grateful to have them. All I wanted was the sex and the chance to experience something new—to explore this new curiosity Astor's desires had created in me.

I knew I would miss Astor, but I didn't think I could fall in love with him. He was my total opposite. He had no qualms about being rude to people, and I couldn't bring myself to be offensive to anyone. He thought of himself as higher on the scale than most, while I knew where I stood on the totem pole of life—somewhere in the middle, not nearly as high up as he thought himself to be. And that was good. That would be what would save me from falling in love with him.

Knowing that Astor and I could never really make each other happy—other than sexually—actually made me feel a lot better about the affair.

After taking my time shampooing and conditioning my hair, I got out of the shower to dress in my uniform. I left my hair wet when I put it into the mandatory bun. I wanted the fruity scent to waft past Astor's nose; I wanted to see his eyes when he caught my smell. I liked the way I could arouse him with just my scent alone.

As I walked out of my room, I noticed a few eyes turning to look my way. Donny wore a shit-eating grin as he said, "Good morning, Sunshine. Did you have a nice night?"

"I did," I said as I made my way to the front door.

"I know." He laughed, and Ariel joined in the laughter.

I didn't care if they knew what I'd been up to with Astor. "You won't have to worry about the noise anymore. I'm about to take him up on his offer to stay with him in his bungalow."

Ariel looked shocked. "You're what?"

Donny shook his head. "Nova, you should really think about what you're doing. You'll basically be living with this guy—and you hardly know him. And what's going to happen when summer's over and he has to leave?"

It was a pretty personal question, but Donny and I had become pretty good friends since we both arrived on the island. I indulged him. "We both know this will end when he has to leave." I thought my coworkers were sweet to care about me. "He's a busy man. Even if he did ask me to leave with him, I'd be alone most of the time. I would hate that." I wrinkled my nose at the thought. "It's just a summer thing; we both know that."

"Have you asked Mrs. Chambers if this will be okay with her?" Ariel asked, her eyes wide with concern.

"No." I put my hands on my hips as I thought about that. "There are no rules that forbid this though. But maybe you're right—I should run this by her first. Thanks for caring, you guys. See you later."

I headed to see Camilla on my way to tell Astor my decision. As I walked up to Camilla's private quarters, I saw her coming out the door. "Oh, hi, Nova. How are things going?"

"Really great." I skipped a few steps then stopped, feeling silly. "I want to ask you something."

"Sure, walk with me. My husband's coming in, and I'm going to meet him at the dock." She looped her arm through mine, and we headed toward the dock where all the guests arrived. "What do you want to ask me?"

"Well, Astor has asked me to stay with him in his bungalow for the rest of his stay here. I wanted to make sure you're okay with that before I tell him anything." A twinge of nerves moved through me. I'd never even thought about the fact that I might not be able to do what he wanted.

Camilla stopped then pulled her sunglasses off to look me in the eyes. "Has he told you what he's into?"

She'd surprised me completely. "How do you know about that?"

She put the glasses back on and started walking again. "Because he and I belonged to the same club a few years ago. Have you ever been somebody's submissive, Nova?"

"No." I was glad she had asked—I was eager to talk to another woman about this. "But I want to learn. At least I think I do. He's given me the option of stopping any time I want to."

"He has to give you that option. You're the one who's really in control, after all." She smiled and leaned in close to whisper, "I'm a Sub, too."

"Really?" I asked, feeling a little shocked.

"Yes, my husband was my Dom. I met him at the club Grant owned—the one we all belonged to." The way she smiled told me the memories were happy ones. That smile made me feel so much better about being Astor's Sub.

"Is there a similar club on this island, Camilla?" I had to ask.

"Might be." She laughed before pulled me along to hurry as we heard the distinct sound of a boat approaching. "He's almost here!" She stopped as we came near the guest bungalows. "Okay, you can stay with Astor if you want. And you can come to me if you have any questions about this. Never feel like you have to do anything you don't want to. For this kind of relationship to work, you need to be honest with your Dom at all times. If something hurts—more than you want it to—tell him. I know the man knows what he's doing, so you'll be safe as long as you let him know your limits." She kissed my cheek. "Now, go tell him the good news. I've got to meet my husband or I'll have my ass handed to me." She laughed again as she let me go and hurried to get to the dock.

I looked over at Astor's bungalow for a moment, taking a deep breath and trying to calm the butterflies in my stomach. I needed to get to it.

As I walked toward the bungalow, I saw Astor come out of it. He waited just outside the door until I reached him. "I made breakfast," he told me. "Care for some?"

Surprised, I tried not to show it. "That sounds nice." I walked through the door as he gestured to it. "I've got an answer for you."

"By the smile on your beautiful face, I bet I know what it is." He came in behind me, closing the door. "And I saw you walking and talking with Camilla. Did you ask her if it would be alright for you to stay with me?"

I took a seat on one of the barstools and reached for a piece of bacon. "I did." I took a bite as he looked at me with those devastating eyes of his.

"And she said what, exactly?" he asked as he came to stand right next to me.

Inhaling his unique scent—musk and lime—I sighed as I thought about getting to fall asleep with that aroma in my nose. "She said that you guys used to belong to a club. She asked me if I knew what you're into. And she said that if I need any advice, I should go to her."

"Sounds like you told her your answer before you told me." He walked away from me with a frown on his face.

"I kind of had to." I didn't like what I read in his body language. Getting up, I went to stand behind him as he opened the fridge, getting out some coconut milk.

When he turned around, I was blocking his path. He looked down at me. "So, tell me what you told her, Nova."

"Can I have a hug first?" I asked as I stretched my arms out.

When a smile curled his lips, I had to smile back at him. "A hug, huh?" He laughed as he shook his head. "That's not what this is about. Do you know that?"

He put the carton on the counter and wrapped his arms around me as I snuggled into him. "I know this isn't what it's about. But that hasn't started yet. So I can have this, can't I?"

Hugging me tightly, he kissed the top of my head. "And when will *that* begin?"

I liked the fact that he was giving me this control. "Camilla explained things to me, and I feel confident about this now. So, this can begin as soon as you want it to. I'll let you decide that, Astor." I emphasized that statement with a cheeky wink.

"How kind of you, my little love slave." He kissed the top of my head again, and then groaned a little. "You're really going to test me, aren't you?"

"I certainly will try." I looked up at him. "And I'll try to learn everything you have to teach me, Astor. I want to experience this with you. I never thought I'd want such a thing, but I do want this with you."

"And only me." His eyes narrowed as he looked at me. "Only me, Nova. I'm fiercely protective of what's mine. And you will be mine from this moment on, right up until the second I leave this island. Only after I leave will you once more be free to do what you want. Until then, you will do only as I say. Any infractions will cost you. Do you understand?"

"Cost me?" I asked as I took a step back. "What does that mean?"

"It means you are allowing me to have complete control over you and your actions. If you do something I don't like, it will warrant a punishment." He pulled a sheet of paper out of the drawer behind me then placed it on the countertop. "Sign this after you read it. And then it will begin."

When I saw the words *Dom/Sub Agreement* at the top of the page, my legs went weak.

Shit! This is really happening!

12

ASTOR

"Y ou put July thirty-first on this contract as the ending date." Nova looked up at me with worried eyes. "You said if I didn't like it, we could stop doing it."

Being new to the lifestyle, I should've expected Nova would have some questions about the Dom/Sub contract I'd written for us. "There has to be an ending date as this isn't an open contract. If you read further, you'll see the stipulation about pulling out of the contract anytime either of us wants to."

"Oh." Her hazel eyes fell on mine. "You think that you might want to end this before it's over?"

"One never knows." I liked the way her brow furrowed. She didn't like to think that I might not being satisfied with her. But I thought it best that she should worry about keeping me pleased.

"I see." She looked back at the document, continuing to read it thoroughly, just as I'd told her to. "And here it states that I will allow you to do anything you want to my body, but nothing that will leave permanent markings or scars." Shaking her head, she simply said, "No. That's not okay with me."

"You want me to leave marks and scars?" I laughed, knowing she didn't mean that. "See, I know how to make jokes, too."

With a frown, she let me know, "That's not funny." Her long finger tapped the paper. "There are some scary words in here—words like knife-play. I'm going to need you to explain that to me before I sign anything."

"Not a problem." I took a seat on the sofa. "You see, I like to cut the clothes away from my Sub's body most of the time. It gets the blood pumping." The look on her face made me very happy—the bit of fear there sent a shiver down my spine and straight to my cock. "Gently scraping the blade over the skin makes endorphins rush around in the body. And lots of moving endorphins means great things, sexually speaking."

Nova got up, coming to sit at the other end of the sofa with the document in her hand. "Under punishments, it states that you can do various things. One of the things I think is pretty cruel is not allowing your Sub to climax if she's done something you believe she needs to be punished for."

I liked how hard she was thinking about every clause in the binding document. "Don't do anything to make me decide to use that as a punishment then."

Placing the paper on the sofa between us, she asked, "What types of things would make you want to do that to me? And how would that punishment occur? Would it mean that we simply wouldn't have sex of any kind?"

"No." I ran my finger over the back of her hand as she laid it on top of the paper. "It would mean that I would take you to the brink of orgasm time and time again, making you feel as frustrated as you would've made me by not following my orders."

"So tit for tat," she mused with a smile. "I can see that. I don't feel I've got anything to worry about then. I've never frustrated anyone in my life. I'm easy to get along with." I had to fight to keep a grin from spreading over my face; the woman had done nothing but frustrate me since the moment I met.

Looking the rest of the document over, she nodded. "Yeah, I'll sign this." She picked up the pen and signed the paper before handing it over to me. "Here you go. Your turn, Astor."

As I signed my name heat stirred in me. "You're mine now, Nova. You know what that means."

With a smile, she nodded. "Yes, I do. You get to do with me what you will."

Pointing to the floor in front of me, I gave her my first order. "Drop your clothing on the floor. I want to inspect my Sub."

"You can't be serious," she said as something akin to horror filled her expression.

"I am." There was no time like the present to start teaching her what it meant to be a Sub. "You're mine now. You belong to me. I want to inspect your body and let you know what I want you to change about it."

"As if I can change anything about my body, Astor!" But even as she spoke, she got up and began taking off her clothes, folding them neatly and placing them on the end of the sofa.

"Good girl," I coaxed her. Once she was down to her bare ass, I circled the air with my finger. "Turn all the way around, nice and slowly."

Although sighing heavily, Nova did as I told her, moving in a slow circle so I could get a good look at her. "Is this slow enough, Master?"

"I don't like being called that. You will call me by my name. But I am your master whether you call me that or by my name." I wanted to really look at her body and see if there were any places that needed toning or tanning. "Raise your arms and turn around once more."

"And what are you looking for now, Astor?" she asked as she followed my orders.

"Never mind." I stood and put my finger to her lips. "You're to do as I say without complaint. No asking questions about everything I tell you to do."

Her throat moved as she gulped. I knew she felt uncomfortable. "Yes, sir."

Running one finger over her pink lips, I whispered, "Good girl." My cock strained against the fabric of my shorts. Looking at the sunlight streaming through the open glass doors, I thought it might be time for some privacy.

I closed the doors then took the remote, closing the shutters and shrouding us in dim light. Nova stood perfectly still as I set the remote down and went to my bedroom to retrieve something I knew would frighten her.

Coming back with a belt in hand at my side, I saw the look of fear in her eyes just before she closed them. "Clasp your hands over your head, Nova." I hadn't told her she could put them down yet. I had no desire to spank her, however.

Using the belt to bind her hands, I walked behind her, nudging her to the door of the bedroom where a hook was set to hold a robe. Looping her bound hands overhead, she was forced to stand facing me on her tippy toes.

With her body stretched tight, I ran my hands over every straining muscle, loving the way trails of light came in through the tiny spaces the shades allowed. Parts of her skin glowed, while the darkness masked others. "You are truly remarkable, Nova. There's isn't one thing that needs to be changed to improve your appearance."

"Thank you." Her cheeks blushed as she looked away.

I took her face between my hands. "Don't be embarrassed by your perfection."

"I'll try not to be." She smiled. "It's just that I've never thought of myself as perfect."

"What do you think is wrong with your body?" I asked.

"My toes are kind of long," she said. "Nothing can fix that." Her eyes went to look at her belly button. "And my belly button is almost an outie."

I moved my hands down her sides and sank to my knees in front of her. "I think it's cute." I kissed her in the place she felt self-conscious about, and she moaned as goosebumps pebbled her creamy flesh.

Kissing my way down one leg, I kissed each toe she'd deemed too long. I didn't find a problem with a single one of them. "You're making me feel so good, Astor."

"You're making me feel good, too." I kissed my way up the other leg then stopped as I came to her hip. Pulling her legs apart, I kissed her sweet pussy, loving the heat that already radiated from it.

The sounds she made were exquisite as I kissed her deeply and intimately. Blowing on her clit, I licked it a few times, making it swell with arousal. Then I moved my hands behind her knees, lifting her legs and placing them over my shoulders, finally appeasing the sizzling hunger I'd had for her for way too long now.

One long, continuous moan came from her as I ate her like she was the best meal I'd ever had. She was mine now. All mine. Every part of her tasted that much sweeter, knowing that I could have any part of her that I wanted—at least until the end of summer.

But I would have my fill of her until then. I could leave the island knowing that I'd had the best of her. No one would ever get from her what I had gotten. My mission was to spoil her for other men. I wanted to leave her with memories that no one could ever compete with.

She might meet another man, fall in love, and even get married, but she'd never have a man who made her feel as good as I could— who would do the things to her that I would.

Her legs tightened around my neck, and I knew she was about to let it all go. I wanted more this time. I moved her legs, pulling her down off the hook. "Knees, now."

I had to help her get on her knees as her legs were wobbly and the belt still held her hands together. As soon as I bent her over, I dropped my shorts and slammed my dick into her tight pussy, making one hellacious groan as I did.

Her pussy clenched around my cock in a hard embrace. It took only three hard thrusts before she came all over my cock. Hot juices poured all over me, even running down the insides of her thighs. I couldn't stop myself. I moved harder and faster, wanting more from her.

Her soft ass felt incredible every time I went in balls deep, my thighs rubbing against her silky cheeks. As soon as I felt the first trickle of cum leaking from the tip of my cock, I pulled out of her— even though it was the last thing I'd wanted.

My need for her had come on too fast, and I hadn't put on a condom yet. I was forced to spill my hot seed on her back as I growled with frustration. "Fuck!"

Although her legs quivered, Nova stayed as still as she could while I stroked my hands up and down my cock to release as much cum as I could. I would fuck her sweet pussy again as soon as possible. But next time I'd use a rubber. I wanted to feel her cunt clamped around my climaxing cock the next time, and every time after that. I'd never wanted anything more.

What the hell is wrong with me?

13

NOVA

L ying in an exhausted heap on Astor's bed after hours and hours of the most intense sex in the history of sex, I knew I'd made a colossal mistake. "I can't stay here with you, Astor."

"You're kidding, right?" He threw one arm over my limp body in an attempt to keep me right next to him. "You signed the contract. You'll do as I say. And I say stop thinking about leaving my bungalow." His lips pressed against the side of my head, and I turned in his arms to look at him.

The way his dark waves hung around his face made him look even more handsome. I brushed back a chunk of hair that fell in front of one sea-green eye. "Astor, I don't think I can do this with you. I'm afraid."

"You are not." He grinned at me knowingly. "You didn't bat an eye when I used the belt to bind your hands. You moaned with anticipation when I raised my hand to slap your ass. You cried out for me to spank you harder and harder. You're not afraid of much, I can tell you that already."

He mistakenly thought I was talking about being afraid of the things that go along with a BDSM relationship. I wasn't. "I am afraid.

Not of any of that. I was never really nervous about the BDSM stuff, I just didn't think I'd like it. But what you've done so far has proved me wrong."

A growl made his chest rumble against mine. "And there's so much more to show you, my angel."

I didn't know if I should tell him the truth. I did want to see what else he could show me—what else he could do to me to send me into a world of unimaginable pleasure. But my heart had begun to get into the mix, and that seemed like a bad thing. Especially so soon into this relationship.

Trailing my fingertips over his bearded cheek, I whispered, "I'm afraid of how my heart is enjoying this just as much as my body."

His eyes closed, his grip on me went loose. "You've got to learn how to keep your heart closed. This is sex. Not love."

"I know that." My head began to hurt as if my brain knew that what he wanted was impossible. "If I sleep with you through the night, then I think I'll start to see this thing between us as more than what it is."

"This is the first time I've ever tried to do this with anyone who wasn't already practicing this lifestyle." He looked into my eyes, seeing me for who I truly was. "You're fairly innocent about sex. But you're especially innocent about how it all works. Sex is just a thing, an activity, not an emotion the way love is. I make your body feel good. You make mine feel good. That's it."

"You don't like me?" I asked. "You don't like holding me?"

"I adore holding you." He kissed the tip of my nose playfully. "I like holding your body. Your gorgeous, soft, supple body. It's nothing more than that. And it shouldn't be any more than that for you either. You don't really know me."

"I do, too." I knew it sounded childish, but I felt he wasn't giving me enough credit. "I accept your brusque demeanor. I bet you've had a hard time finding women to accept you the way you are."

"You're right." His eyes moved away from mine to look at the sunlight that trickled through the shutters of his bedroom. "Tell me why you kept putting up with me. And be honest."

After thinking about it, I had to admit, "It's my job."

"Yes." He grazed his lips down my neck. "You wouldn't like me in the real world were we to meet as just two strangers. You would get tired of me—want to change me. We would fight, and I would end up walking away from you. I know exactly how all of that would play out. That's why I want things to be simple. No love. No hard feelings. Just enjoy what we have here. It can't last."

"You're probably right. You can be an incredible ass." I smiled at him to lessen the blow. "But you sure know how to please a woman."

"Thank you." Slowly, he moved toward me until our lips met. We'd kissed and screwed more in one day than I had in my entire life. Yet somehow, when his lips touched mine, lightning jolted through my body, right down to my very core, filling me with electricity.

His cock began pulsing against my stomach as our kiss grew more passionate. I'd been exhausted just seconds earlier, but the kiss renewed my energy, and I gripped him tightly, pulling him to move his powerful body over mine, wanting him to take me one more time.

Spreading my legs as he moved, he settled between them. His hard cock pushed into my sore tunnel, the twinge of pain lasting only a moment before my body welcomed him in.

Slow and easy, his strokes kept me moaning with desire. Astor invoked desire in me in a way no man ever had. I knew we had more than just a physical attraction for one another. I saw the way he looked at me, or rather gazed at me, at times when he thought I wasn't paying attention.

Astor did like me—more than he would admit, I was sure. And I liked him, despite his arrogant ways. Somehow, I could see past all that nonsense. Not that it was a charade, because I knew Astor was that kind of a man—the kind who speaks his mind even when it's not appropriate.

In a way, I liked the abrupt way he spoke. I always knew right where I stood with the man at all times. No need for guessing when it came to Astor Christakos. He let you know what he thought, no matter how unpleasant.

And he thought he and I would be able to have crazy hot sex for a few months, sleep together—our bodies entwined—then give it all up. And maybe he would be able to. But what about me?

His lips left mine to move up my neck in a soft line of kisses as I trailed one foot up the back of his leg. This time was different. No demands, no punishments. This was making love—a thing I'd never done before.

Moving my hands along his muscular back, I memorized each hill and valley there. His soft beard tickled my skin as he delivered tiny kisses up and down my neck before taking my earlobe between his teeth and biting me with a gentle tug.

His breath was warm in my ear as he said, "I like this very much. You're extremely receptive, baby."

Arching up to him, I murmured, "You make it easy."

I ran my fingers along his shoulders then down to his massive biceps, which bulged as he held himself up off me just enough so he didn't squish me. Squeezing the muscles with both hands, I let out a little groan at how great they felt.

So much muscle, so much power, and yet he took me so gently that it made my breath catch. Our previous sexual experiences hadn't been this gentle, but now that I knew he could handle me this way, I knew I would want to end every day like this.

He moved to give some attention to the other side of my neck, and our eyes locked for a second. He smiled at me—an actual smile that made me feel so special. "Nova, I very much enjoy the way our bodies react together."

Running my hands up to wrap my arms around his neck, I pulled myself up to kiss him. My lips nearly touched his, but not quite. "I very much like you, Astor Christakos. Very much." I kissed him, and the groan that escaped him gave me chills.

He'd told me not to think about love while we had sex, but I couldn't stop myself. I loved the way he moved. Loved the way our smells combined. Loved the way his damp hair hung around his gorgeous face. I loved it all.

I loved him.

Pressing my head back against the pillow, he began moving faster as he kissed me harder. I felt him become more demanding, and I moved with him as he sped up his pace.

His mouth left mine, and he looked at me with narrowed eyes. "Shit!"

"Shit?" I gasped.

Yanking his cock out of me, he let his load out all over my stomach. "I forgot to put on a condom."

Panting with excitement, I laughed. "Seems you did forget that."

Looking frustrated, Astor rolled off me and went to the bathroom. "I'll get a towel and clean you up. We need a shower. But if you get up with all that on you, you'll make a mess."

I looked down at the cum on my belly and moved my legs a little, realizing how very wet I was down there. And *I* hadn't had the chance to have an orgasm.

But he'd turned me on so much with the way he'd taken me, I was pretty sure it was just my own juices. He'd pulled out in time.

I hope.

Getting pregnant would put a real damper on our sexy summer. So I decided not to even mention anything to Astor as he wiped his cum off my stomach.

"There you go. Now, come. Let's shower, get something to eat, and then we'll come back to bed and sleep the night away."

I didn't say anything as we showered, but my mind was a million miles away. I was preoccupied by thoughts of him holding me in his arms all night.

Even as I made us a couple of ham sandwiches for dinner, all I could think about was his body next to mine as we slept—and what might happen in the middle of the night. And what might happen to my heart once we were done.

After dinner, I cleaned up, then worked up my courage to tell Astor what I wanted. "I know you want me to stay." I looked down, knowing he would protest and not wanting to get into an argument.

"But you want to go back to your place," he finished my thought. "You're afraid your feelings will get involved if you sleep with me." He paused for a moment, his eyes scanning my body. "I could make you stay if I wanted to. But I felt your heart when we were in bed being easy with each other. I saw it in your eyes, too." He took me by the chin, lifting my face to look at him. "I liked taking it slow like that, but you need to know that even that—the tenderness—baby, that was just sex, too."

"It was more than that to me. You can't keep trying to convince me that I don't know what I'm feeling." I closed my eyes. "I don't think I can do this, Astor. I don't think I can separate things the way you can."

"You can learn." He kissed the top of my head. "I have faith in you. And I also know that you'll be bidding me goodbye with a smile on your face when I leave. I'm a lot to take. I know that about myself. You'll be glad to be rid of me by the end of this."

It started to grate on me, the way he thought himself unlovable. "As hard as you must think it is for a woman to fall in love with you, I'm afraid you might be wrong. I will see you in the morning, sir. Bright and early, as always."

I left him then, feeling his eyes lingering on me as I went. Astor could think what he wanted. Although inexperienced in the world of sex and love, I knew what I felt for the man. And I could see he felt something more for me as well.

Too bad nothing can ever come of it.

14

ASTOR

S itting on the deck, I watched the waves roll in. *Alone.*
Nova had once again decided to go back to her room after our day of torturous fun. She'd been doing that for the last couple of weeks.

She'd expressed interest in visiting the island's private club, but I'd told her she wouldn't like it. The truth was I knew there would be other people there ogling her body—and I didn't want that.

Jealousy had never been an issue with any of my other subs; the fact that I was feeling it now didn't sit well with me. That's the main reason I let Nova go home each evening after dinner.

Although she'd kept her thoughts to herself, I could see her emotions in her eyes. She did still seem to care about me, much more than I thought she could. I thought the rush of tenderness she'd felt after our first evening together would've worn off by now, but it seemed I was wrong.

But I wasn't being the real me while on vacation. I'd taken a more laid-back approach to life. I knew it wouldn't last when I got back to work.

Nova had monopolized my time. I hadn't even cracked open my laptop since arriving. She'd changed every plan I'd made—except for my rigid morning exercise routine. I had an addiction to that that she couldn't change.

But if she'd stayed the nights with me, then I might've forgone my usual exercise routine for one of a more sexual nature. Only, Nova never wanted to stay with me. And I didn't want to make her.

As I sat there watching the moon rise up over the silver-colored ocean, I thought about Nova. She came to mind even when she wasn't around. Another thing that had never happened with any of my other women.

No woman had ever wholly captured my attention the way Nova had. I tried to tell myself it was just a result of the vacation; I didn't have anything else to worry about, so why not think about her all day? It wouldn't last once I went back to work.

But maybe if it did, then I'd need to start thinking about her in a different way.

Strolling out onto the deck next to mine, I saw Grant staring at the moon. "Hello, neighbor."

He looked at me and nodded. "Evening, Astor." He looked back at my bungalow. "She left you again?"

"I let her go." I didn't want him to think the Dom in me had gone soft. "She's trying her best not to get too invested, the poor girl. Keeps saying she's worried she'll fall for me—but frankly, I can't see how she could fall for me."

He nodded as he looked back at the moon. "Yeah, I used to think the same thing about Isabel. I was such a beast."

I didn't know a lot about Grant's personal life, especially his life with his wife, but I knew he'd been the owner of a BDSM club, and she had worked there for him. I could imagine their relationship would've been somewhat rocky.

"I'm not quite a beast." I thought about how to describe myself best.

But then Grant did it for me. "No, you're not a beast. You're more of what I like to call a *difficult* personality. But the thing about you is, you tell it like it is. Like it or not, you put it out there. You're honest.

To a fault, but you are honest. Maybe she likes that about you. Or maybe she just likes the way you fuck her."

"Talk about being honest to a fault," I said and then had to chuckle. "I don't think it's just because of the way I fuck her. Nova liked me before we ever got physical. But now that we have, I think she's mistaking the way I make her feel for love for me."

"And how do you feel about her?" he asked.

He'd stumped me. I didn't know exactly how to put into words the way I felt about her. But I did know that things would change when I got back to my normal life. "For now, she's always on my mind. But I know myself. When I get back to the real world, that will change. Nova will fade into the background. Hell, she may even disappear. Who knows?"

Grant nodded. "Who does know?"

Isabel called out for him, and he waved at me before heading inside to her. I thought about how it would be if Nova were around. Would I be sitting out on the deck? Or would I be inside, cuddling with her in bed as we watched the moon rise?

The melancholy brought on by my thoughts didn't make me feel good at all. I decided I needed to make things different with her. If I stayed on this path, then we would both end up getting hurt.

I got up and went to bed, rising the next morning with a new agenda where my little submissive was concerned.

She met me in the kitchen after I'd showered. "Good morning, Astor. I thought we'd do something different today. There's a boat leaving in an hour. It'll be an all-day excursion with dolphin watching and snorkeling."

The plan I'd had in mind had been much different. I'd been thinking about treating her like the Sub she was. But her eyes were all sparkly as she talked about the boat, and I didn't want to dim that light.

"Okay, sounds good to me." I picked up the coffee she'd placed on the counter for me, then thought I might add, "You know, most subs don't tell their Dom what the day's activities are. Most of them leave that up to their Dom."

"I'm not trying to learn how to be submissive to anyone else." She placed a plate with ham and eggs in front of me as I took a seat at the bar. "And you know you can always tell me no."

"And take that light out of your eyes?" I picked up my fork to dig in. "Never. You've been hounding me to do one of these excursions since I got here. I knew I would have to give into you one day or another before I leave here."

"We only have about a month left. I figured we could do both activities in one day—kill two birds with one stone. I knew you weren't likely to take two days to do both." She made herself a plate then took the seat next to me. "There's a chef who'll be coming along with us. He's going to make some scrumptious food as we take our tour. I can't wait!"

Her excitement couldn't be masked. "I suppose I should've taken you up on this some time ago. I had no idea it would make you this happy, Nova."

Sipping her coffee, she smiled. "In the beginning, you didn't care to make me happy. I'm glad you care to now."

The day hadn't started off the way I'd intended. I'd wanted to set the scene for the rest of my stay, playing the Dom to the max. Obviously that wasn't quite working out. I felt a frown furrowing my brow.

How can she come in here and just change everything? Why do I allow her to do this?

I looked at her out of the corners of my eyes, finding her taking a bite of ham. When a smile pulled my lips without me realizing, I felt my heart pounding in my chest.

This isn't good.

Nova picked up her coffee, looking at me. "Astor, you've never told me about your family. Do they live in Athens, too?"

"Yes." I looked at my plate, trying not to focus on her. I seemed to be doing that way too much lately. "I'm the oldest of six children. My two brothers and I are all older than our three younger sisters."

"Like the Brady Bunch," she said, then laughed a little. "Only I assume you all have the same mother and father, unlike those kids."

"Brady Bunch?" I asked, not having a clue what she was talking about.

"Yeah." She put her cup down, focusing her attention on me. "That old television show with the three boys and three girls. The mom had the girls, the dad had the boys. They got married and made a family of six. You know, that show."

"I don't watch television." I watched as a frown took over her expression.

"Ever?"

She kind of made me feel stupid for a brief moment. "We didn't have a television when I was growing up. I do have them in my home now, but I never really sit down and watch them. There're always so many other things to do. When I'm working, I am really working. My days are filled with meetings, and when I do get home, it's usually just to shower and sleep before getting up and doing it all again the next day. I'm a very driven man."

"Yeah, I can see that." She looked at her half-full plate, then picked it up as she moved to clean up.

"You're not hungry?" I asked. "Did you eat at your place before you came here?"

"No." She cleaned her plate off, scraping the leftovers into the trash bin. "I guess I've just lost my appetite." A long sigh escaped her. "I suppose I've been romanticizing you a bit. In my imagination, you're surrounded by your family. Your life is full of love and happiness, not work and more work. Do you and your family live together?"

"My parents and brothers, with their wives and children, do live at my home. My sisters live with their husbands." I finished my food and took the plate to her as she did the dishes. "But I'm hardly ever there. I travel more often than I stay home. And even when I am in Athens I spend most of my time at the office."

"You are a busy man, aren't you?" she asked as she took my plate from me.

"I am. I've told you that. Are you just now letting that sink in?" I smacked her on the ass. "I've never been untruthful with you."

"You're right. You haven't been dishonest in any way, Astor." She put the dishes in the drainer then wiped her hands on a dishcloth. "And it would be unfair of me to ask you to change."

I ran my hands over her narrow shoulders. "Nova, I'm sorry I can't be who you want me to be."

"You're doing pretty damn good at it right now." She leaned in to wrap her arms around me, hugging me.

"This isn't the real me, though. That's what I keep trying to make you see." I had to keep telling her that. She had no idea who the real me was.

"I like you this way, though." She looked up and kissed me on the cheek. "Would it be so hard to let yourself be like this in your regular life, too?"

"It doesn't matter. If I took you back with me, you would end up hating me. At least this way, you and I can part ways on good terms. We'll have memories we can cherish with no bad times to mar them." I kissed her sweet lips and felt them quiver against mine.

I'd made her cry and hadn't even meant to.

15

NOVA

"What do you mean, let's get in?" Astor asked as I dangled my legs over the side of the boat, splashing the water with my feet.

"Let's swim with the dolphins." I had a feeling he'd jump in if I did. But before I could jump off, he had me in his arms. "Astor!"

"You're not jumping in." He carried me to a seat, sitting me down. "Are you crazy?"

"They won't hurt anyone." I looked over the side at the six dolphins who'd come to the boat, just as curious about us as we were them. "I've swam with dolphins before in Florida. It's fun."

"Well, you're not going to do that in front of me." He took a seat next to me. "What if one of them bites you?" He leaned over and nibbled my neck. "You are rather tasty, you know."

Giggling as his beard tickled my neck, I moved away from him. "They won't bite me. Come on, Astor. I try all sorts of things that you want me to."

Pulling his sunglasses down, he looked at me. "None of those things endanger your life."

"I hardly think swimming with dolphins can be considered life-endangering." Glad to be wearing sunglasses myself, I rolled my eyes.

"Why do I have the feeling you're rolling your pretty hazel eyes at me, Nova?" He ran his finger along my cheekbone. "Do you think I'm overprotective of you?"

"Right now, I do." I leaned way over the side to entice the dolphins to swim up to me.

Astor leaned over, too. "Are you trying to pet one of those things? Don't do that."

Extending my arm to reach out, I laughed. "Come on, Astor. Look." One came up to the surface with a happy squeak. "He wants me to pet him." I placed my hand on the tip of his snout, showing Astor that there was nothing to be afraid of.

"Do those things carry diseases?" he asked as he looked at the cone-shaped teeth. "And that thing's got a lot of teeth. Stop touching him. Nova."

"He likes it." I splashed a little water at Astor, teasing him.

"How do you know it's a he anyway?" Astor leaned in closer to me, putting his arm around my waist and holding me as if he were afraid I would jump in.

"I don't know that for sure." I sat back up as the dolphin went to join his friends. "When I see any animal, I usually call it a *he*."

"Well, stop playing with them. Let them go on their merry way. I don't get what all the hype is about anyway. They're big fish that play with humans more than other sea creatures. Big deal." He pulled me to sit on his lap. "You want to play? Play with me."

"You sound jealous." I liked that. "And they're not fish."

"Mammals, I know." He smiled. "Just testing you."

"I've lived in Florida my whole life." I kissed his cheek. "Of course I know they're mammals. So, what's your favorite mammal, Astor? Horses? Pigs? Bears? Dogs?"

"You're my favorite mammal, Nova." He kissed my lips, softly and sweetly. "You're my favorite everything."

My heart felt like it swelled in my chest, so much it almost hurt. "I am?"

"Of course you are." He kissed me again. "I want you to know that.

I've had more fun with you than I've had in my entire life. I'll always cherish this time with you."

"Me, too, Astor." I leaned my head on his shoulder. Knowing I only had a few more weeks with him had me feeling blue, missing him already. "You know, I'll get a two-week vacation around Christmas. I usually go to my parents for the holidays, but I could come to see you. You could take a holiday, too. We could—"

His lips pressed against mine, stopping my words. Then he eased up on the kiss, pressing his forehead to mine. "Nova, please don't. You know I can't."

"Sometimes it feels like I'm messing around with a married man, Astor." I got off his lap and went to get us a couple of bottles of water. "Why do you act like there's no way in the world we can ever see each other again?"

He took the water I offered and shook his head, making his dark waves graze his broad shoulders. "I don't want to keep you hanging on like that. I want you to feel free to move on."

"I don't like it when you talk like that." I hated it actually. "You move on after someone dies. You don't move on when the person you care about goes someplace else to work. We could keep in touch—through phone calls or Skype or e-mail. We could meet up now and then. There's no reason to think we can't continue our relationship, albeit long distance." I flopped on the chair across from him then took a drink of the water.

"I'll be busy." He replied flatly.

"Every minute of every day?" I asked. Before he could answer, I went on, "I think you're afraid of falling in love with me, too, Astor."

"Afraid?" He laughed as if the idea was implausible. "I am not afraid. What I am is sure that love cannot last between people who live apart. Especially when one of those people is so busy that it defies the other's imagination."

"I guess you're right. I won't bring it up again." Maybe it was time to put all this silly love stuff behind me and accept the inevitable as Astor had been telling me all along. Astor would leave in a few weeks and life would go on. "I'll have many more guests to tend to. You'll keep traveling all over the world. Who knows what fate has in store for either of us?"

He didn't say a word. Not a single thing. Instead, he put his hand over the side of the boat, trailing his fingers in the water. I watched as a dolphin swam up behind him without Astor noticing.

When it squeaked at him and moved under his hand, Astor touched the creature. "You're not slimy at all."

I watched him in silence as he looked at the animal that'd come to say hello. Astor's fingers moved gently over the grey skin. And then a big splash from another dolphin broke the spell, showering us both.

Laughing, I got up and got a towel to wipe myself off before wiping the water away from Astor's soaked face. "It's hot anyway. It was nice of them to shower us with water and cool us off. Don't you think?"

The way his hands slipped down my sides to rest on my waist made me all warm inside. "Is it wrong of me to hope that I don't think about you after I leave? Is it wrong that I don't want to think about you tending to another male guest? Is it wrong to want to put you out of my head once I've got to leave you?"

I hadn't thought about it like that. "No, I guess it's not. Not if it'll bother you to think about me. I can see that." I gulped down my emotion, trying to stay composed. "I do hope you'll remember me sometimes. Just focus on the times when we were like this and not what I might be doing without you. But you should know that you've probably ruined me for other men." I kissed him lightly. "Who could possibly replace you?"

"That's nice of you to say. I will take that with me when I go and pretend you're alone in your bed at night, dreaming only of me." His lips grazed my cheek. "I never want to think of you in some other man's arms, much less in his bed."

It didn't matter if he never said those three little words to me; I knew he loved me then. And I wouldn't add the weight of those words to his heart, either. He knew I loved him; he didn't need to hear it.

But he did need more from me. And I needed more from him, too.

If all we had were a few more weeks, then I needed to make as many memories as I could. They would be all I would ever have to remember him by.

"Tomorrow, we should do something crazy." I moved with him to take a seat as the captain started the boat.

The captain's voice came over the speakers, "If you'll take your seats, the chef has informed me that he's almost ready to serve lunch, which we'll enjoy on the deserted island just ahead of us."

Black cliffs jutted out of the blue ocean water on one side of the island. Astor looked ahead. "How about we do something crazy today and jump off one of those cliffs after lunch?"

"I was thinking about going parasailing." I eyed the tall cliffs warily. "But if you do it, I will."

"We'll do it together." He smiled at me as he took my hand. "I'm in, Nova. Let's do some things we've never done before—things we'll never do again with anyone else."

I'd been in the hospitality industry forever. In all that time I'd never had a summer fling. Perhaps that's all this was. A summer fling destined to burn brightly—then end.

Later, as we held hands and jumped off the lowest cliff I could find, I found myself full of joy. Living in the moment was so much better than mourning the inevitable loss of Astor before he even left.

We ate dinner on the boat that night, then went ashore heading to his bungalow. Astor steered me past the pier that led out to the overwater houses. "I'll walk you home, Nova." He put his arm around me. "It's been a long day, and I'm sure you're tired and want to get to bed."

"I am tired. We had an eventful day, didn't we?" I leaned my head on his shoulder as we walked through the sand, barefoot.

"We did. What do you think about just chilling out tomorrow?" he asked.

I smiled at the way he'd said chilling out—it was so unlike him. "That sounds good to me. We can make more crazy memories after we recuperate from today."

Stopping at the door to the staff housing, Astor kissed me on the cheek. "Good night, sweet prince," I whispered.

"See you tomorrow, my angel." He turned and left me, and I watched him go before turning to go inside.

Floating to my room, I showered then changed into a pajama set before climbing into bed. But as tired as I was, I couldn't seem to keep my eyes closed. My bed felt so empty, lying there alone. And I wondered if that's how Astor had been feeling without me in his bed.

We both wanted to make the most of this time we had together—to do crazy things and make lasting memories. With our earlier conversation ringing in my ears, I got up and put on a thin robe before heading back out. Walking in the dark, using the moon's light to guide me, I went to Astor's bungalow and used my key to slip into his room.

Soft snores told me he was fast asleep. That didn't stop me. I wasn't there to do anything other than sleep in the man's arms.

He didn't wake when I eased onto the bed. Slipping in beside him, I pulled his arm to wrap around me, snuggling back to spoon against him. "This feels nice," I whispered.

Astor nuzzled my neck, pressed his lips against my ear, leaving a small kiss there. I had the feeling he knew I was there, but neither of us said a word.

And I prayed that my heart wouldn't break into too many pieces when it was all over.

16

ASTOR

Honeysuckle grew all around me as I walked through a garden. Birds chirped as they flew through the clear, blue sky. Somewhere not too far away, the sound of waves lapping at a shoreline could be heard.

A butterfly flew by my face, tickling my nose with its wings. I rubbed my nose with the back of my hand, laughing. Then the sound of someone's quiet snores had me looking around to see where the sound came from.

A sudden stab of pain in my stomach made my curl in on myself, clutching at the spot where someone had hit me with their elbow. My eyes opened, and all I saw was blonde hair. Moving my head back to take stock of my surroundings, I found Nova in my bed. Her elbow, nestled uncomfortably in my stomach, told me she'd woke me up with the jab.

By the sound of her soft snores, she was still fast asleep. I thought it had been a dream when she'd come in last night. Thankfully, it was real.

After moving her arm out of my gut, I ran my arm around her, nuzzling back in and loving the honeysuckle scent of her hair. I couldn't recall a better morning. Waking with her in my arms felt better than I'd imagined.

Although she shouldn't have snuck into my bed without my permission—any other Dom would've been pissed about such disobedience—I loved that she'd made the decision to come on her own. I'd wanted her in my bed for a long time, and hoped this meant she would be staying with me the rest of my nights on the island.

The snores stopped abruptly then her body stretched as she groaned. "Are you awake back there, Astor?"

Kissing her neck, I whispered, "I am. Thank you for coming." I hugged her tightly. "I thought that had been a dream last night."

She turned in my arms to face me, smiling as she took my face in her hands. "I wanted to see this handsome face first thing in the morning. I knew you'd still be devastating even when you first wake up." She kissed me softly. "I didn't bring anything, so I've gotta get back to my room early, before anyone wakes up and catches me running around in my pajamas."

I held her tight. "You're not going anywhere. I'll go to your room and gather your things. You can take a shower while I do that."

Blinking at me, she shook her head. "This is so not what I thought being a submissive would be like."

"I'm supposed to take care of you, Nova." I kissed her cheek. A small part of me never wanted this to end. I never wanted to let her out of my bed. I could just lay here with her forever.

But then the rational part of my brain began working again. The part that knew I would never be okay with doing nothing all day. Nova filled my time, I enjoyed being with her, but I knew eventually the bug would hit me. I would get a new idea and want to run with it, leaving Nova behind. I thought it much better to leave her behind in Paradise before that happened, rather than drag her with me somewhere just to lose interest.

"I'm getting in the way of your morning exercise routine, aren't I?" She tried to pull herself out of my arms. "I'll go shower so you can get to it. I didn't mean to mess up your schedule."

"I can think of another way to get my exercise." I held her still. "If you'll be so kind as to allow me to use you as my weights."

She looked a little worried. "How will you be doing that?"

"Trust me?" I asked her, knowing she did trust me fully.

She nodded, but the look on her face let me know she was still skeptical. "Yeah, but I don't want you to drop me. I'm not super light."

"I think I can handle you." I sat up then pulled her to lie across my lap, running my arms underneath her. "Tense your body up. Lie as straight as a board," I directed her.

She did as I said, and I lifted her up, doing curls with her body. "Ha! This is crazy, Astor!"

"Count them off for me, baby. I do fifty of these." I'd never lifted up a girl like this before. I found it surprisingly stimulating, and before I knew it, my cock had perked up, no longer wanting to be left out. "I'm thinking some pushups should come next."

Her eyes went wide, and she bit her lower lip, looking down at my erection. "Uh oh."

Climbing off the bed, I took off my pajama pants. "Strip."

Taking off the shirt and short pajama set, she cocked one brow. "And what should I do now?"

"Lie back, spread those long, lean legs of yours and let me do the rest." I moved between her legs, holding myself up off her. "Bend your knees up toward your shoulders and guide me into you when I come down. I can take it from there."

She laughed as she guided me into her, but that laughter soon morphed into a glorious moan, "Oh, Astor!"

"I'll count these. You can just lie there and enjoy yourself." I began counting as her eyes closed.

She placed her hands on my biceps, squeezing my muscles as I pushed myself up and down. "Oh, this is nice. Is this how every morning will be with you?"

"Fifteen," I counted. "Yes, this is pretty much how it'll be. Sixteen."

Since I hadn't put on a condom, I wasn't about to let myself get too into it. The counting made it easier to think about the burning muscles of my arms and legs, rather than the pleasant sensation of my dick sliding in and out of Nova.

But when she began to shake and moan with her impending climax, I couldn't keep my head out of it anymore. Her tight cunt clamped around my erection, and I lost all focus on anything other than fucking her.

I forgot about the pushups and went straight to work, thrusting as hard as I could as she came all over my hard cock. "Astor!" she squealed as I slammed into her sweet, hot pussy that dripped with juices for me.

Her hard climax showed no signs of stopping and I kept moving, loving the way her body held mine so tight—like it never wanted to let me go. "God—damn it! You feel so good, Nova!" I grunted as I tried to hold on.

Panting like animals, we fucked hard. Her nails dug into my back, and I growled with satisfaction as she screamed, "I can't stop coming!"

"Don't stop, baby. Give me all you've got!" I rammed into her harder.

Never in my life had I so badly not wanted to pull out, but I had no choice as my dick gave in. "Shit!" I pulled out of her and spilled my cum all over her belly. "Fuck!"

Her eyes still closed, she moaned. "Damn, babe."

Having no choice but to roll off her and go get a towel, I felt frustrated that so many of our encounters ended like this. "Why the fuck aren't you on the fucking pill?" I didn't mean to bark at her, but my blood was still on high from all my exertions.

"I'm sorry," she said quietly. "I suppose I can go see the resort doctor and get on birth control today."

"Nova, it doesn't work that damn fast. I'm leaving in three weeks. It won't even kick in before that time." Grabbing a towel, I tried to calm down. This wasn't her fault—it was mine. "I'm sorry. I should've taken a minute to put on a rubber." I went back to her side and rubbed the towel over her stomach. "I'm sorry. Ignore everything I've just said. I was just frustrated—I wanted to stay right where I was. I hate pulling out of you."

"It's okay." She looked a little shocked by my outburst. "I understand. I felt frustrated, too."

Turning to go back to the bathroom to take a shower, I went on, "I can't make any mistakes with you, Nova."

She sat up, looking at me. "What does that mean?"

"We can't get pregnant." I stopped to look at her. I wanted her to know how seriously I felt about this. "I don't have time for a girlfriend, much less a kid."

"I know." Her head dropped, and I could tell she was sad about the whole thing. "You don't have to explain anything to me. You don't have time when you work. I don't exactly have time to have a baby right now either. We're on the same page about this." She got up and walked toward me. "I don't want to have a baby with a man who doesn't have time to be a father either, you know."

She moved past me to start the shower as I tried not to be offended by what she'd said. But the truth was, I was. "So, you would want a baby if I had time for you and a kid?"

With a laugh, she stepped into the shower, letting the water wash over her. "Astor, let's not pretend. You've been very honest with me this whole time. You're going to go back to work, and you're going to forget all about me."

"I never said I would forget about you, Nova." I hadn't said that to her, but that girl knew me better than I knew myself, it seemed.

"Okay, *forget* is too strong a word." She filled her hand with shampoo then rubbed it into her hair as I began to brush my teeth. "You'll push me to the very back of your mind. You'll pull me up only when it suits you. Like maybe when you're masturbating. Then, when it's over, you'll put me right back where I was."

Rinsing my mouth, I knew better than to get into this further. What was I supposed to say? She was most likely right. Walking into the bedroom, I found a T-shirt and laid it on the bed for her before going back into the bathroom. "I've put a T-shirt on the bed for you to wear until I get back with your things."

"Only bring one set of clothes. I don't plan on bringing all of my things here." She rinsed her hair, then got out of the shower.

Handing her a towel, I stepped into the shower myself. "I wasn't going to bring all of your things. That would be stupid. There're only..."

"Yes, I know," she cut in. "Three more weeks." Wrapping the towel around herself, she looked back at me. "And I think I will go see the doctor and get on birth control anyway. It might help make my periods more regular. They're so erratic."

For some reason, the thought of her being on birth control had me feeling jealous. "Are you sure that's the only reason you want to be on birth control, Nova? You never saw any reason to be on it before. Have you been thinking about taking your newfound sexual knowledge and using it on another man?" I'd begun to see red—and didn't like that at all.

"No." She laughed as if the idea was silly. "You sound jealous. That's cute. I just think that being on the pill will be better for me. I've always had weird cycles. I've been surprised more than a few times by Aunt Flo just showing up unannounced."

I knew I couldn't get mad at her for such practical reasoning. Hell, it wasn't any of my business anyway. "I'll shut up. This topic is aggravating me."

"Talking about my menstrual cycle bothers you that much?" she asked with a grin on her face.

"No," I said as I got out of the shower. "Talking about you being with other guys bothers me that much."

So much for remaining unattached. *I'm getting a little nuts over this girl.*

17

NOVA

"**B**reakfast is ready, Astor." I placed the platter of sausages and scrambled eggs on the bar. "I'll let you eat alone this morning and run over to see the doctor while it's still early."

Coming in off the deck, Astor eyed me warily. "No. I don't want you going on any birth control while I'm still here. After I'm gone, do what you want." His eyes narrowed, looking troubled. "It's not sitting well with me, knowing that I'll be leaving you here—alone—with all this sexual knowledge I've given you."

"You're serious, aren't you?" I wanted to laugh, but the look on his face told me it wouldn't be smart.

"Very serious." He took a seat and began putting food on his plate. "So, sit and eat with me, Nova."

I got myself a plate, too, then took a seat next to him. "I was wondering if we could go see that secret club sometime before you leave."

His entire body went rigid, and he turned his head slowly to look at me with wide eyes. "Why in the hell would you want to go there?"

His reaction wasn't what I'd expected. "I thought you might like it. I thought you might be able to show me things there that you can't show me in here."

"And for what?" he asked as he shook his head. "So you can start going to that place when I leave? Get yourself another Dom? Are you crazy?"

"That wasn't my intention, Astor." The man seemed to be getting more jealous as the days went by. "I just thought—"

"Well, just stop doing that." He put his fork down and turned to me, taking me by the shoulders. "Look, this isn't easy for me. I've never liked anyone as much as I like you. I've never enjoyed anyone's company the way I enjoy yours. It's not going to be easy to leave here. And if I know for a fact that you're on birth control and have been introduced to that sex club...it will drive me crazy."

I couldn't help the smile that crept over my lips. "You know what? I like that. You really are going to miss me, aren't you?"

"No." He let me go and went back to eating.

"What do you mean, no?" I asked as I watched him pick at his food, something I'd never seen him do before.

"I'll be able to put you in the back of my mind." He looked at me. "But only if I'm not worried about you screwing someone else. If I think about that, I'll never stop thinking about you. You know what that will mean, don't you?"

"That you love me?" I asked then winked at him before picking up my coffee and taking a sip.

"Nova, don't." He looked at his plate then stabbed a sausage as if it were a rabid beast. "You know this isn't about love. This is about having the most relaxing time of my life, and then getting back to work."

I'd been wondering something for the past few days but hadn't wanted to ask at the wrong time. The time had come, though. "Astor, do you think you'll come back next summer?"

Putting his fork down, he looked at me with a stoic expression. "Who knows?" His expression suddenly changed to one of worry. "If I come back, will I have to see you with another man? Because I'm really worried that might happen."

How can I know the answer to that?

Blinking at him, I didn't know what to say. But the look on his face compelled me to say something. "If I know you're coming, I will make sure I'm not with anyone. If you can promise me that you'll come back next summer, I'll wait for you. I won't see anyone else—but only if you promise to come back to spend the summer with me again." I crossed my fingers at my side, hoping he would make me the promise I wanted so badly.

I hadn't been planning on asking him such a thing. But now that I had, I hoped he would tell me he'd come back to me. I would be fine as long as I knew he'd come back to spend three more months with me. I could deal with that.

But he shook his head. "I can't make you any promises, Nova. I won't do that to you. I have no idea what's ahead for me. I don't want you sitting here pining away for me. I also don't want you with other men, but I can't have everything, can I?"

"You could," I said with a snarl. "If you would just commit to coming back next summer, you could have what you want. I wouldn't be with anyone." I lowered my voice, not knowing when I'd started shouting. "I only want you, Astor. Can't you see that? You managed to make time for a vacation this year. Why can't you just make it a plan for next year, too?"

"Because I can't." He got up, leaving his plate half-eaten. "How can you not understand this?"

I got up to follow him. "I guess I can't understand because lots of people have relationships even when they can't be with each other all the time." My hands flew up in the air in frustration as I followed him out to the deck. "People in the military have relationships. Some even get married right before being deployed."

He spun around to look at me. "Is that what you want, Nova? You want me to marry you? Leave you here while I go back to business as usual? And what? Only see you once a year for three lousy months? Does that sound like any kind of a marriage to you? Because it doesn't sound like a good one to me."

"You act as if it's so black and white, Astor." The fact that he'd assumed I'd want to marry him had pissed me off. "And have I ever said I wanted to marry you? You've never even told me that you love me. Why would I ever expect you to marry me?"

"You don't want me to say those words to you, Nova." He turned away from me. "You think it's going to be hard to part ways now, let's add love into it and see what happens."

I didn't think it would be half as bad as he clearly did. But then again, I thought he could make time for us if he wanted to—but he seemed to think that was impossible. It hadn't been my intention to argue this morning; we didn't have time for things like that. "Look, let's drop this. It's pointless anyway. You're leaving. I'm going to let myself believe you're never coming back. End of discussion."

Turning to walk back inside, I felt his hand on my shoulder, stopping me. "Don't think I'll never come back. Who knows, really? I might."

"Why would you say that? That's not fair." I looked at him over my shoulder. "You're making me crazy, Astor."

"You're making me crazy, too, Nova." He turned me around and pulled me into his arms. "I guess we'll just be a little crazy for a while. Once I leave, things will get back to normal for both of us. Life will go on."

"As if we'd never even met," I whispered.

He pressed his lips against the top of my head. "I'll never forget you. Don't think like that." Then he held me away from his body, looking at me with a stern expression. "But I want you to promise me that you will never go to that club. Not all Doms are like me. I don't want to think about you being hurt. Promise me that, and I won't ask you to promise me anything else."

"I don't even want to go if it's not with you anyway." It was an easy promise to make. "I promise I will never go to that club or seek another Dom, Astor."

"I'm going to hold you to that, Nova. I do have Galen's number. I can find things out about you, you know. Don't make me come back here and beat someone's ass over you." He smiled, but I believed he might do just that if it came to it.

I didn't think it was fair that he could talk to his friend about me, but I didn't have anyone to tell me about him. Maybe Galen would see fit to speak to me about what Astor got up to. Who knew for sure?

But it was more likely that I wouldn't want to know what the man was up to anyway. Maybe Astor would find someone who ran in the same circles he did. Whatever circles those were. Maybe once our time together was over, he'd want something more permanent with someone whose schedule was more compatible with his. He might even find some rich, hard-working woman who had a hard time finding the room to have a relationship, just like Astor did.

My mind was taking me on a journey I didn't need to go on. I needed to distract myself before I went nuts. "Wanna go for a swim?"

"Huh?" he asked, looking a little confused. "One minute we're talking about your future as a Sub, and the next you're wanting to swim?"

Pulling my sundress over my head, I dropped it on the deck then jumped into the water in my bra and panties. "Yeah, I want to swim." I needed to get out of my head and away from that conversation. It was better for both of us if we didn't talk about what we would and wouldn't do once he left me.

Astor dropped his shorts and my jaw dropped with them. Totally naked now, he jumped in after me. I laughed as I tried to swim away, but he caught me, pulling me underneath the deck. "Come on. I've got an idea."

Pushing me against one of the pilings that held up the deck, he yanked both sides of my panties, ripping them off me. "Oh, God!"

His cock pushed into me hard, knocking my breath out of my lungs. "How the fuck you can make me so hard while we're arguing is a mystery."

I wrapped my legs around him, loving the way he fucked me hard and fast. The water splashed around us, but no one could see what we were doing.

My fingers curled into his flesh as I laid my head on his shoulder, whimpering with desire. I had to be quiet in case anyone was walking by, but it was difficult. Astor made me feel more feminine, more desirable, than I'd ever felt before. He brought out this little sex goddess that I'd had no idea lived inside of me.

I didn't want to put that part of me back to sleep once he left the island. But I also didn't want to show that part of me to anyone but Astor.

If things had been different, I would've loved exploring that side of me with Astor every day. But I knew there was no use in trying to figure out how we could keep on seeing each other. He didn't want to make the effort to figure anything out anyway.

In a way, it made me mad that Astor refused to even think about how we could keep seeing each other. It wouldn't be hard for me to visit him every now and then, and I'm sure he'd be able to stop by the island occasionally as he traveled around the world. But he was so damned bullheaded, determined that I wouldn't like the person he became when he was engrossed in his work.

Could work really be more important than love?

Even though he wouldn't tell me he loved me, I knew he did. And I loved him, too, but I wasn't going to tell him that, either. I suppose I was as stubborn as he was in that sense. But I preferred to think he was the more stubborn out of the two of us.

I had to bite down on his shoulder as an orgasm took me off guard. He groaned as he held himself back from joining me. "Fuck, I've got to pull out again. Why do I keep doing this shit to myself?"

What a great question.

Why do I keep doing this shit to myself?

18

ASTOR

Nova and I had managed not to talk about my leaving for the last few weeks of my stay. We'd gotten along a lot better, leaving that subject off the table.

With only one night left, Nova and I decided to go out for dinner. I didn't want to make her cook, wanting to cater to her on our last night together. "And bring us some champagne, too, Petra." I watched Nova's eyes go wide with surprise. "Alcohol, Astor?"

"Why not?" I reached across the table to take her hand. "I don't think it'll kill me to have a little. You've made sure my workouts were extra strenuous, after all."

I loved the blush that covered her cheeks. "I suppose I have."

The waitress came back with a bottle and two glasses. "I've got to tell you, Mr. Christakos, island life agrees with you. You're nothing like the man I met when you first came here. I hope we'll see you again soon." She looked at Nova. "I'm sure your hostess would like to see you again, too."

Nova stopped smiling as she looked at the other woman. "I know you mean well, but please stop talking, Petra."

"Oh," she said awkwardly, seeming to understand Nova's abruptness. "I see. Well, enjoy the food and drink." With a wave, she left us alone.

Picking up a glass, I filled it and placed it in front of Nova. "It's part of her job to try to get guests to come back. But I'm not going to let that start any kind of talk that might lead to an argument."

Nova took the glass in her hand as I filled one for myself. She held it out as she made a toast. "To a summer I will never forget."

I tapped my glass to hers. "To this summer."

We took sips and then placed the glasses on the table. I looked up to find Nova gazing at me. "You know, you really have changed, Astor. I'm proud to say that I had a hand in that miraculous transformation."

"A hand?" I knew it was all her doing. "I'd say there was a bit more than that. You've brought out a side of me I had no idea was there."

"You've done that for me, too." She picked up her fork to start eating her meal of seared scallops drenched in garlic butter.

I'd been keeping Nova holed up in my bungalow most nights, but I had plans to take her out after dinner. Galen had brought in a stand-up comedian, and he'd asked me to attend the final performance; he thought the man was hilarious and had been badgering me to see for myself.

"Galen wants me to go to see the entertainment tonight." I hadn't told Nova about that yet. "What do you think about that?"

She cocked a brow at me. "Are you asking me to join you? Or are you telling me that you want to go alone?"

"I want you to go with me." I knew I wasn't adept at asking women out, but I had no idea I was that bad at it. "I suppose I could've worded that differently. You may have smoothed out a lot of my rough edges, but you haven't managed to make me any better at flirting or making moves."

She frowned at me. "Good. I didn't want to make you better at those things."

"Seems I'm doing a fine job of saying the wrong thing this evening." I took a drink. "Best to keep my mouth shut."

"No, it's okay. I'm used to it." Nova laughed and speared a scallop, holding it up to me. "Taste this. You'll love it, I promise."

"There's a lot of butter on that." I shook my head.

"It's your last night of vacation, and you're already drinking alcohol. Go ahead! Live a little!" She held out the fork again and I took the bite.

It melted in my mouth, and I nodded as I moaned. "It is good."

"You want another one?" she asked coyly as she went for another.

"No. Just knowing how it tastes is good enough for me. I've got to get back to my normal habits soon. Best not to spoil myself too much."

I knew that would be easier said than done. I would have a hard enough time dealing with the loss of the woman I'd grown so comfortable with. Nova had made my nights beyond compare. She'd filled my days with fun and so much joy that it made leaving her the hardest thing I'd ever had to do.

But I would do it. My mind was already racing with what would be waiting for me when I returned to my office in Athens. But as Nova's hand moved over mine, I forgot all about Athens and work. "Is it okay to say that I'm going to cherish tonight?"

"It is." I pulled her hand up to kiss it, then placed it back on the table. "So, what kind of activities will keep you busy after we all leave?"

"We'll have a meeting tomorrow evening after all the guests have left. I think we're getting a week off, and then more guests will be coming. Paying guests who won't get the one-on-one attention Galen's friends have gotten." She smiled at me. "I won't be anyone's personal host, just so you know. It'll be my job to make sure everyone knows about all the activities here."

"Good." I didn't want to think about her entertaining anyone else. There was one thing I did want to think about her doing after I left— but that was a secret. Nova wouldn't find out about that until after I left the island.

"I'm going to go to Florida to visit my parents during my week off." Nova looked at me over her glass as she took a sip. "Miami," she went on. Reaching into the small clutch she'd placed on the table, she pulled out a small piece of paper. "My cell number and the address to my parents' house are on this. Of course, once I come back to Paradise, my cell won't work. If you want to talk to me, you can call the resort here, and they'll deliver a message to me. Then I can call you back if you leave a number."

I took the paper and put it in my pocket. I knew I wouldn't call her. I couldn't do that to her or myself. "If I need it, I'll use it."

She looked at me as her chest rose and fell, taking a deep breath before asking, "You don't want to give me your number?"

"I don't know what good it would do," The truth was that I didn't want to pick up the phone and hear her voice. It would only make things so much harder for me. But I didn't want to have to say that to her. "If you really need me, you can ask Galen to contact me."

"And what if I can't reach him, Astor?" Her eyes looked a little wild, and that concerned me. "He's leaving when you guys do. I don't know when he's coming back. I don't have the man's personal number." She looked down for a moment before looking back at me, taking another deep breath, steeling herself. "You know what? I don't need your number. It's okay. I'm sorry for bringing it up. I know you want this to be cut and dry. No loose ends. Forget I mentioned it. Let's just have a good night. It's our last one, and I don't want to say or do anything to ruin it."

Wanting to put the whole thing behind us, I was more than happy to forget about everything she'd said. "Well, the comic performing tonight is supposed to be hilarious, according to Galen. I hope I get his humor. You know how I am with jokes."

She tried to put on a smile, but I saw the sadness behind it. "I'll explain it if you don't get it." She laughed, but it came out weak. "If I get it." Leaning her chin on her hand as she rested her elbow on the table, she broached a new subject. "So, tell me what it is that you do, Astor. I've never understood what it is that keeps you so busy."

"I'm an investor, for the most part." I actually enjoyed talking about what I did. I'd never brought it up with Nova because my work was what would keep us apart. I knew she must think about my work as her enemy, the one thing that could take me away from her.

But she actually looked interested. "So, that's how you made your fortune then, investing in the ideas and inventions of others?" she asked. "Or do you invest in stocks and bonds and things like that?"

"Galen and I got to know each other when we were still in college. As you know, that man is a genius and has come up with so many inventions and business ideas that I've lost count, as has most of the world." I sat back, picking up my glass as I thought about my first endeavor.

"I had saved a little over five thousand Euros by the time we'd finished college. Galen only needed a little bit more money to get his hovercraft off the ground. In the first year of sales, my investment had multiplied by one thousand. And I went from there. I met more and more inventors and helped them make their ideas a reality."

"And the money doesn't hurt either," Nova said.

"It's a nice byproduct." I wondered if she'd even understand the real reason my work was so special to me. "I know I wouldn't have gotten to meet the people I have if I didn't have money, but I would do everything for free if I could. The world doesn't work that way, unfortunately. Money makes it all happen, so I do make money off my investments. That way I can help bring more ideas to life. Plus I've got the pool business, too. Someone else does the running of it now. I only work on special projects, like the pools and waterscapes for this resort. All of it keeps me busy, but I love every minute of it."

"You do sound passionate about it." She looked at me, and I could see the jealousy in her hazel eyes. "It's the most impassioned I've ever heard you sound."

I retook her hand. "Come on, I've spoken pretty passionately to you, haven't I?"

A blush stained her cheeks once more as she ducked her head. "Yes, you have." She looked back up at me. "I just mean that you really do love what you do, and I can see that. I'm not going to lie and say I don't wish it took up so much of your life, but I'm glad you love what you do. And I'm happy it makes things happen for other people, too."

I knew Nova deserved more, and I gave it to her. "I've been able to travel all over the place to meet with people who need my help. And once they tell me their ideas, I'm right there with them to watch it all come together. I'm not the kind of investor who simply hands over money and doesn't care if their idea works or not. I love seeing the final product.

Last year, I went to Africa. A doctor there had this idea of making an artificial pancreas to help people with severe diabetes." I sat back as I recalled the nature of that product. "I saw a lot more blood and guts than with most of my investments, but in the end, the doctor did complete the product. It's not out yet. It's still got to go through all kinds of trials, but it's real now. Someday, maybe someone you know will need one of those things, and you can think of me when you hear the news."

"I'll be thinking of you pretty often, Astor. I can assure you of that." She picked up her glass and took a sip through trembling lips.

I had to give it to her; she was one of the toughest women I'd ever known. Being able to hold it together while wanting to break down wasn't easy.

I knew that because I was struggling, too.

19

NOVA

I'd already returned everything I'd brought to Astor's bungalow back to my room in staff housing the day before he had to leave. When I woke up that morning, his arms holding me tight, I felt sick to my stomach and had to hurry out of bed to get to the bathroom.

My stomach churned, and my head was killing me. I blamed it on the glass of champagne I'd had during dinner the night before. And when I actually threw up, I made fun of myself as I washed my face. "Lightweight. A few months without any alcohol and you go and puke over one little drink." After getting it all out, I felt a lot better and went back to bed.

Astor sat up, rubbing his eyes with the back of his hand. "You okay, baby? Did I hear you get sick in there?"

I climbed back under the blanket, snuggling in next to him. "I'm sure it was the alcohol. I feel much better now."

He looked at me with a worried expression, then put his hand on my forehead. "You weren't even tipsy last night. I can't believe you'd have a hangover from it."

"It's been a few months since I've had any alcohol. My body must not be used to it." I pulled his arm around me again. "Don't worry about it. I feel fine now."

He settled back into bed. "Okay. But if you feel bad later on, promise me you'll see the doctor. You might have food poisoning or something. I don't want it to get out of hand if you do. If anything happened to you..." He stopped talking.

How would you know if anything did happen to me?

I didn't say that. I didn't want to end things on a bad note. My plan for the day was to spend as much time with him as I possibly could. He'd said his yacht would be picking him up just before lunch.

I didn't want to think about it. I just wanted to lie there with him and fall back asleep.

We slept in that morning. I didn't think either of us wanted to start the day—the day that would be our very last together. No more nights of intense sex. No more days of fun in the sun. Nothing. It would all be over soon. All that was left were the goodbyes.

I'd made a pact with myself—I would not cry. Not until after Astor left. I wouldn't make him feel guilty for getting back to his life. He hadn't come to Paradise to fall in love. He'd come for a temporary getaway, and that was all. I couldn't expect him to stay, or take me with him, or even keep in touch.

When the sun made it impossible to stay in bed any longer, we got up. Astor pulled me along with him to the shower. "How about we have a little fun in here, baby?"

I thought that sounded great—the water would hide my tears. "Yeah, sounds fun."

As the warm water washed over our bodies, he pushed me against the tiled wall then thrust his hard cock into me one last time before pulling it right back out. "You know what? Let me grab a condom. I'm not about to pull out this time."

I laughed even though I really wanted to cry. I knew he wanted the last time to end well.

Hopping back in the shower with the condom already in place, he got right back to where we'd left off, his cock sinking into me as I wrapped my legs around him.

I leaned my head on his shoulder, letting the water trickle down my face, washing the tears that poured from my eyes down the drain with the rest of the water. My heart ached so bad that I had no idea if I would make it through the day.

"I've had the best time, Nova. I really mean that." He kissed my neck, then sniffled a little.

Knowing he was crying, too, broke me.

Astor, don't leave me.

I couldn't say the words though. I couldn't do that to him. He'd never lied to me. He'd never pretended things could go past this day. So how could I tell him that it was killing me to let him go?

I loved him. I never wanted to hurt him. I never wanted to make him feel bad about leaving me to get back to his life. I would never do that to him. *Not ever.*

At least I knew that he really did love me. His sniffles told me more than words could ever say. This wasn't easy for him either.

Our bodies moved together for the longest time. Neither of us wanted it to end, and we took our time, lost in each other. We knew this would be our last time together.

My nails raked his back as I came, leaving long red welts in their tracks. His teeth bit into my neck, leaving his mark on me as well. We both knew those marks would only last a few days. But the memories of our summer together would last forever.

Neither of us wanted to eat anything that day. As I packed his things for him, I found a handful of my own things that I'd forgotten to take to my room. "I should run these to my place. I'll be right back. It's almost time for you to go."

He grabbed my hand as I passed him. "Wait."

Looking back at him, I tried not to cry. "I'll be right back, Astor."

"Why do I keep thinking that you aren't going to see me off, Nova?" he asked with bleary eyes.

Shaking my head, I tried to think of what to say. I couldn't tell him he was wrong. I didn't want to say goodbye. I didn't want to stand there while the damn boat took him away from me.

If he'd been coming back, even in a year, I think I could've done it.

But the fact that we most likely would never see each other again made it too hard to take. The fact that I would probably never hear his voice again made it too much to bear.

Swallowing hard, I tried to put on a brave face. "As hard as this is, I will be there to say good..." I had to stop talking as a knot formed in my throat. I couldn't say the word.

"Goodbye," he said. He ran his fingertips across my cheek so lightly. It felt like a feather brushed across my skin. "You will be there to say goodbye to me, Nova. Even though it's killing you inside, you will do it for me. Won't you?"

Nodding, I pulled away from him, then ran out of his bungalow to take my things back to my room and collect myself. Tears blurred my vision as I ran toward staff housing. I tried so hard to hold it all together but just couldn't do it.

Thankful that no one was around when I got to the building, I hurried to my room. My stomach was rolling again, and as soon as I got inside, I had to run to my bathroom to puke.

I sat on the tile floor afterward then fell to my side and laid there, wishing this day had never come. I didn't want it to end. And I knew I would never, ever have anything like this with anyone again for as long as I lived.

I finally staggered to my bed and fell on it. I knew I had to pull myself together. Astor would come looking for me if I didn't get back to him soon. Collecting myself and gathering my energy, I washed my face, pulled my hair back into a tight bun then walked out of my room.

Kyle walked in the door just as I went into the living area. "Hey, Nova. I just put my guests on their boat. I heard that your guy's is coming in the next half hour."

My hands began to shake. My stomach churned, and I ran to the kitchen, Kyle on my heels. "I'm gonna be sick!"

I made it to the trashcan just in time. "Shit, Nova!"

I could barely breathe when I was done, and Kyle helped steady me so I didn't fall. "That's the third time today." I made my way to the sink to wash my face again. "I don't know what's wrong with me."

Kyle wet a paper towel then placed it on my forehead. "I know I'm getting personal here, Nova. But your guy is about to get on a boat and get the hell out of here. So, I think I should ask this. You and he have been having sex, right?"

I felt my cheeks heat with a blush. "Yeah. What's your point, Kyle?"

"Have you two been safe?" He took me by the chin and looked into my eyes. "Every time?"

"Yeah." I looked away then looked back at him. "Except..." I grabbed him by the arms so I wouldn't fall down. "Kyle!"

He looked at me as he shook his head. "One time is all it takes, Nova. Have you been missing your monthly...you know?"

"It's always been erratic." I shook my head, not believing it could be true. "But I haven't had one all summer long. It's not that rare for me though."

Taking my hand, he pulled me along with him to his room. "Don't judge me, Nova. But I came to this island fully prepared for the worst possible situations—there aren't any drug stores here in Paradise. Thank God I don't need this, but you might." He pulled me into his room with him before sitting me on his bed. "Wait here. You need to take this test before that man of yours leaves."

"You have a pregnancy test, Kyle?" I asked, feeling more than a little surprised.

"I have several of them." He pulled a brown paper bag out of his closet then dumped a dozen of them on his bed next to me. "Take your pick."

Gulping, I closed my eyes and picked one. "I'll take this to my room."

He shook his head then pointed at his bathroom. "In there. If it's positive, then you might need a shoulder to cry on and someone to take you to the daddy-to-be to make sure he does right by you."

I froze. "No. If I'm pregnant, you can't ever tell him, Kyle. You can't tell anyone who the father is. Promise me!"

He gave me a stern look. "We'll talk about this after you take the test." He pointed at the bathroom door again, and I went in to find out what my fate would be.

The test seemed simple enough. Pee on the stick then wait a few minutes. I did it just the way the instructions said. And then I saw a plus sign and fell against the door.

"Shit!"

20

ASTOR

T hirty minutes passed, then an hour. I sat on the deck, waiting for Nova to come back to me.

She won't let me go without saying goodbye.

Would she?

I'd seen the sadness in her hazel eyes, the downward tilt of her pink lips. She didn't want to say the words. Just as I didn't want to tell her that I loved her, just before leaving her for good.

Who would ever understand that loving her meant leaving her alone?

But I knew myself, and I knew what I had to do. Nova had changed me, but only for a little while. Underneath the sadness at having to give Nova up, there lay an excitement for what waited for me at my office.

If I could change my ways for good, live the island life forever with her, then I would. But I knew I couldn't do that. What would be the use of staying until we hated each other?

At least this way we still had love in our hearts for each other. No bad times to tarnish our memories. We'd remember only the good times, to cherish and love and hold them in our hearts for the rest of our lives.

Who knew, I might get tired one day and want to cut back on work. If that ever happened, I would find Nova again—if that's how things were meant to be.

My watch chirped, altering me that my yacht was nearly there. A porter had already come to take my things to the dock. All that was left was to walk there. And I guessed Nova had decided she couldn't make that walk with me.

Getting up out of the lounge chair, I ran my hand through my hair then over my beard. First thing I'd have to do when I got back would be seeing my barber and getting myself back in working order. Caveman wouldn't cut it.

As I walked through the bungalow for the last time, I ran my fingers over the bar where we'd sat and eaten many a meal this summer. I looked longingly at the sofa, a place we'd had sex too many times to count.

Then my eyes went to the floor where I'd taken her on her hands and knees. The kitchen counter where I sat her down and eventually bent her over to take her from behind. And then there was the bedroom; I could just see a glimpse of the bed we'd pretty much worn out.

My heart had never felt so heavy. My mind had never felt so numb.

I left the bungalow and walked toward the dock. Just as I stepped off the boardwalk, I looked back toward the staff building. Several people walked near it, coming and going. But none of them had blonde hair. None of them had a perfect silhouette that sparkled in the afternoon sun. None of them were her.

Shoving my hands into my pockets, my head hung low. I just couldn't believe she wouldn't come to see me off.

I wanted to see her face just one more time. I hadn't memorized every little bit of her yet. Or had I?

I knew the three tiny lines that appeared at the outer corner of her left eye when she smiled. The brow over that eye arched slightly more than the right one. Her left breast was a fraction larger than the other. Her left hand held mine tighter than her right one, too.

We'd spent so much time in the sun, her tanned skin had gone one shade darker than when I'd first met her. Her toenails were pink right now—painted by me the day before as we'd sat on the deck of the bungalow, just basking in the sun and each other's company.

Never had anyone so thoroughly entertained me just by being there with me. I would miss her. I knew I would.

My feet moved slowly toward the dock where my yacht and captain waited patiently for me. "Afternoon, Mr. Christakos. I hope your holiday went well."

"It went better than expected, Douglas." I stopped and turned back to make sure Nova wasn't coming.

I stared for what must have been a tad too long as the captain cleared his throat. "Should we be going now, sir?"

Before I turned around to leave, a shadowy figure came out of the jungle, waving a long arm at me. A man seemed to be flagging me down. "Astor!"

Galen had come to see me off, at least. I should've known he'd do that. "Galen, have you come to say goodbye?"

He made his way to me, the sun finally moving out of my eyes so I could see him. "I am. Did ya have yourself a good time, my friend?"

"I did. Thank you for the invitation." I shook his hand as he reached out to me.

He pulled his shades down to wink at me. "Ya leaving Nova here, huh?"

"I am." I looked away, back toward the place I thought she might come from. "I think it's for the best. You know how I work, Galen. It leaves no time for anyone."

"Aye." Galen nodded in agreement. "Are ya comin' back next summer?"

"I really don't know." I'd wrestled with the idea but had never come to a conclusion. "I suppose I'll see how I feel when the time comes."

"How is she?" he asked me. "Did ya leave her crying?"

"She left me." I shoved my hands back into my pockets, fisting them. "I shouldn't have let her go. I had a feeling she wouldn't come here if I let her go back to her room."

"I'm sure she was distraught, Astor." He patted me on the back. "I'm leaving today, too, or I'd keep you updated on your girl."

"She's not mine anymore." I thought about the contract and how it had ended the night before at midnight. "I just hope she stays the good girl she was when I came here."

"I doubt she'll go crazy, Astor. The girl's got a good head on her shoulders." He stepped back, gesturing to my boat. "Well, climb aboard and get the trip home going. She's not comin', and you know that. I'm sure she doesn't want you to see her crying is all."

"She did enough of that in the shower this morning." I thought back to our very last time together, and my heart felt as if it would burst out of my chest and stay right there—in Paradise with Nova. I knew a piece of my heart would always be with the girl.

Galen gently nudged me to get me going. "On the boat with ya. You'll start to feel freer as the distance grows between you two. And you'll know where to find her if you can't get her out of your head. Camilla told me she would be going inland to get some things Nova will need to do that online college you paid for. Nova will be plenty busy doing those classes and earning that bachelor's degree. Did ya tell her that bit of news, Astor?"

"No. I was going to tell her just before leaving, but she hasn't come. Camilla will let her in on that, I'm sure." I felt the paper in my pocket, the one with Nova's cell number and the address of her parents' house in Florida. I had a line to her if I wanted it. "She told me she would have a week off and she'd be going to see her family. I might give her a call next week to make sure she has everything she needs to get her college career going."

"You do what you think is best, Astor." Galen turned to leave. "If I see her, I'll tell her that you said goodbye. But I'll be leaving shortly as well. I'll get in touch with you sometime soon to see how you're doing. Have a safe trip now."

"Are you ready to leave, sir?" Douglas asked me as he noticed my eyes lingering on the land. Apparently I hadn't yet given up hope that Nova would come.

"I suppose so." I went down into the cabin and found the bottle of Scotch I'd kept on the boat for company.

I needed something to kill the pain and poured myself a short glass of the amber liquid. It burned as it went down my throat, straight down to my gut. I sat down on the leather sofa and tried to think ahead instead of dwelling on what I was leaving behind.

Why didn't she come?

How could she do this? Didn't I matter to her? Didn't she love me?

Maybe it had all been an act. Maybe she hadn't meant anything she'd ever said to me.

I looked at the glass in my hand then took another drink. As I felt the boat leaving the dock and entering open water, I went up to check for her one last time.

Stepping out of the cabin, I looked back toward the island. No one stood there. No one was waving and watching me as I left. No one at all.

I wondered what she would have to do to get her mind off me. I knew she cared for me. No matter how much I would've loved to believe it had all been an act, I knew she loved me. That's why she couldn't come to say goodbye. It was killing her to let me go, just as it was killing me.

At least I could leave her with a great education—sexual and otherwise. I just hoped she didn't take the things I'd taught her and teach someone else.

Was it wrong of me to want her to stay celibate for the rest of her life?

I knew it was. But I couldn't seem to help myself.

As far as I was concerned, Nova had ruined me for other women. I was pretty damn sure I would compare any I met to her, and they wouldn't be able to stack up. Nova was incredible; no one could take her place.

The steward came to me, tapping me on the shoulder to gain my attention, which had been stuck on the disappearing island. "I've got lunch ready, sir. Some salmon and asparagus. Would you like to come and eat now?"

"I'm not hungry, Jeffrey. Thank you, though." I saw the surprise in his eyes when I said the words *thank you*. I'd never taken the time for manners or pleasantries before.

"You're welcome, sir. I'll keep it warm for you for when you do get hungry." He turned to leave, then stopped and looked back at me. "If you don't mind me saying so, it looks like you're feeling sad. Would you like to talk about it?"

"No." I took another drink and thought about how Nova would look at me disapprovingly for being so quick to turn help away. But I couldn't talk to the man about her. "Thank you for asking. I am sad about leaving a certain woman behind. But I'll be busy soon, and she'll fall to the back of my mind quick enough."

"I'm sure you will be fine, sir. I'll be in the dining area when you're ready to eat. The chef made a low-sugar low-carb cheesecake. Maybe that'll help." Jeffery left me alone then.

Once the island was out of sight, I reached into my pocket, pulling out the paper with Nova's phone number and her parents' address on it. Crumbling it up, I tossed it into the ocean.

It would only hurt us both if I called her. It would tear us to pieces if I actually went to see her at her family's home.

I had to let her go. All of her. For her own good—and mine.

Goodbye, Nova.

21

NOVA

C old air blew down on me from the vents overhead. The ob-gyn's waiting room was warm compared to the examination room. I was waiting for her, wearing nothing more than a paper robe to keep me warm.

Camilla had surprised us all with a two-week vacation when we'd all expected only a week off. Thankful for that as my head was a complete mess, I hurried home to my parents.

I hadn't told them the news yet. I wanted a doctor to confirm what I already knew deep down before I said a thing to anyone else.

I had so much I wanted to tell Astor. I wanted to thank him for the generous gift he'd left for me. I'd barely spoken at all about going to college online, but he'd taken what little I'd said and secretly talked to Camilla, paying for everything I needed to get my degree. And if it turned out that I was pregnant, I would have to decide whether to tell Astor or not, and then to figure out *how* to tell him if that's what I chose.

Kyle and I had had a long talk before I left the island. He'd helped me come up with a lie I could tell if I didn't want Astor to know about the baby. But that lie would only make sense if I'd gotten pregnant early in the summer—which I'd thought I had.

If I was about two months pregnant, I could get away with telling everyone that I must've gotten pregnant prior to my arrival on the island but hadn't know about it at the time.

Kyle had warned me that not telling Astor might be the worst possible thing I could do, for myself and the child. But he didn't know Astor the way I did. He didn't know how honest and open the man had been with me. His life was busy, and he didn't have time for a girlfriend, much less a baby. Those had been the exact words he'd told me. So how could I tell the man that his worst nightmare had come true?

I still had my fingers crossed that the pregnancy test had been wrong. Three days had passed since I'd taken that test. I'd gotten sick every one of those days. But I missed Astor terribly, and I thought that might be what was causing the puking. I was genuinely upset, after all.

I'd spent the first night alone in my room on the island. Sleeping in my bed alone proved difficult. All I wanted was to feel his strong arms around me, his lips pressed against the soft spot behind my ear, whispering to me that everything would be okay—that he wanted the baby and me.

The next day I'd gotten on a boat and gone to the closest island with an airport. In Aruba, I boarded a plane that took me back to Florida, where my father had met me at the airport and taken me home. The first thing he said to me was that I looked fantastic, and that island life agreed with me. He'd even gone so far as to say that I had a new glow about me.

I didn't tell him or Mom about Astor. I left out tons of details about my time on the island. And I also told them that I didn't know if I would go back or not. They'd both looked stunned by that, and neither understood why I wouldn't want to go back to a place that had made me so happy.

There wasn't a good way to tell them that I might be having a baby, and that I might not want the father to ever know about it. Staying away from the island might be the only thing I could do to make sure I never crossed paths with Astor Christakos again.

"Afternoon, Miss Blankenship," the doctor said as she came into the examination room. "We have the results of your urine test, and I would like to congratulate you on your pregnancy." She smiled at me, but the look in her eyes was one of concern. "That said, is there a father who'll be in the picture?"

Stunned by the words I'd been dreading, I found it hard to breathe, much less talk. My head spun, the room began to sway, and the next thing I knew, I'd fallen back on the table and apparently passed out.

I opened my eyes to a terrible smell, and I tried to wave away the putrid stench beneath my nose. A wave of nausea hit me, and I sat up quickly and tried to jump off the table. Only now, the doctor had a nurse with her, and together they held me steady right where I was. The nurse put a small pink bowl thingy under my chin, which I promptly threw up in.

The doctor looked at me with even more concern. "So that's a no on the father question, huh?"

I nodded and laid back, covering my face with both hands. "This wasn't supposed to happen. We had one slip up. One!"

The nurse came to my side, placing her hand on my shoulder. "It's all going to be fine. You'll see. Things like this happen all the time."

"I'm going to do a pelvic exam to make sure everything's okay in this area. In a few months, we can do a sonogram to let you know how far along you really are. I saw that your last period was four months ago, but you'd said that your cycle is erratic so we can't go by that. If you can give me the date of that slip-up, I think we can give you an idea of how far along you are."

I moved my hands off my face as I thought about the time frame. "The slip up was in late May. The last week, I think. We were on an island in the Caribbean; the days kind of melt together. But I know it was late May."

The nurse smiled at me. "Then the baby will be coming in the middle of February. You're most likely about two months pregnant right now. By the end of this month, you'll be done with the first trimester, and the morning sickness should ease up on you a bit."

Mentally, I calculated how old the baby would be in May, the time when Astor might be back at the island for the summer. Around three months old, he or she might be small enough to not show any resemblance to the man at that age, I thought.

I could only hope the baby took after me when it came to looks, if I decided not to tell Astor.

I honestly didn't know what to do at this point. He'd been so honest with me, and based on the things he'd said, I felt it'd be terrible news for him to hear. I'd meant what I'd said to him all those weeks ago, too. I wouldn't want to raise a baby with someone who didn't even want one—and I don't know if I could do that with someone who didn't want me, either.

I thought about the fact that he had my cell number and even knew where I was staying at the moment. I made a little pact with myself. If he called, then I would tell him. If he didn't, then it would mean that he'd already moved and put me behind him for good.

In the end, the decision was mine to make, but I would let fate play a part in what I decided. If Astor reached out to me before the baby was born, I would tell him about it. If not, then he would never know a thing about our baby.

But I did know one thing for sure at that point, I was going to have Astor's baby. Part of me loved that I would have a piece of that man forever.

"I am happy about having this baby," I let the doctor and nurse know, needing to say it out loud for my own sake as well. "I really am. And I will do what's best for it. I can promise you that."

22

ASTOR

The Aegean Sea sparkled in the afternoon sun as I looked out the window of my office in Athens. Galen sat on the sofa, sipping ouzo.

"I'm sorry it's taken me so long to catch up to ya, Astor. It's been six months since I said goodbye to ya at the dock. Tell me how things have been goin', friend."

I couldn't pull my eyes off the blue water. "I can't lie. The first few months were horrible. I thought I could get back to work and put Nova out of my mind."

"So, she's stuck there, huh?" he asked me.

I turned to see a smile on his face. "Have you spoken to her? Has she missed me?"

"I haven't been back there yet. My plan is to go on the first day of May." He took a tiny sip of the drink.

I wanted to know as much as I could about Nova and what she'd been doing. "Is Camilla still there? Can't you ask her about Nova for me? I want to know if she's alone. Is she waiting for me or...has she moved on? I want to know something—anything—about her. I can't stop thinking about her."

"Call the girl, Astor." He shook his head as if he couldn't understand why I hadn't done that. "Camilla isn't on the island, either. She won't be back until the end of April. I don't know a thing about Nova, and I don't think I should be the one doing any digging on her anyway. You could be doing that yourself, you know. And you know that you can go to that island any time you want to. If the resort is full, you can always stay in my bungalow until May comes around."

"I could, couldn't I?" I walked to take a seat on my office couch, stretching my legs out as I thought about what he'd said.

"You could most definitely do that." He put the glass down and eyed it menacingly. "I think that stuff is already knockin' at my brain."

"Most likely." I rubbed my smooth chin as I thought about going back to the island to see Nova. I wondered if she'd run to me with open arms, or if she'd run away from me instead.

I knew her heart had to be hurting, because mine still ached for her. She might not want to give me the chance to hurt her again. It was never my intention to hurt us both.

I'd honestly thought that leaving was the best thing for us. I thought I could get back to work and she would slowly fade away from my heart and mind. But that hadn't happened at all.

Galen shifted in his seat. "But first, before you do anything else, I need you to come with me to Spain. There's a lad there who's just inherited some land, and he wants to build a resort on it. He's sent me photos and the place has some amazing views. I thought you and I could go see the place and decide if it would be worth it or not."

I was torn about what to do, as I'd just begun thinking about going to see Nova. "Can you call anyone on the island to see if Nova is even there?" I asked.

"I suppose I can if that'll help ease your mind, Astor. I'll call the main line; someone will be at the front desk, I'm sure. They'll know about Nova." He picked up his cell and made the call, putting it on speaker.

I leaned up, propping my elbows on my knees and resting my chin on my fingertips as I tried to hold back the excitement coursing through me. "If you can get her on the phone, that would be even better, Galen. I need to talk to her—need to let her know I'm coming to see her. I need to hear her sweet voice."

"I'll see what I can do," Galen said, then smiled as someone answered the phone.

"Paradise Resort, this is Debbie. How can I help you today?"

"This is Galen. I'd like to know if Nova Blankenship is around?" he said.

I couldn't breathe as I waited, hoping I would get to talk to her. But then the person on the other end of the line said, "Nova isn't here. She's not coming back until May first, sir."

Galen looked at me and shrugged. "Okay then."

"Wait!" I struggled with what to ask next. "Is there any way that she can get in touch with Nova and give her my phone number?"

Galen nodded. "I don't see why not. Debbie, can you send Astor Christakos's phone number to Nova?"

"I don't know how to contact her, sir. I'm sorry." Debbie said apologetically. "The number she left isn't working anymore. But if you care to leave that number with me, I'll make sure she gets it if she calls."

"Yes, give her my number." I got up and walked back to the window, staring at the water again.

Why did she change her number?

Why isn't she working at the resort right now?

Why do I feel like she's slipped away?

Galen related my number to the girl and then ended the call. "Okay, on to what I need from you, Astor. Spain. When can you go?"

I didn't want to think about work at all. But I needed something to take my mind off Nova. "Today, Galen. Let's get the hell out of here and get to work. I don't know what I was thinking. It sounds like Nova's moved on."

Galen shook his head. "You're jumping to conclusions, Astor. You left her money to pay for college; maybe she's not on the island because of that. You never know. She might've decided to go to school in Florida. Debbie said she'd be back in May. You can go to Paradise in May and see for yourself if she's moved on or not."

He was right and I knew that. But something didn't feel right. "I just can't get her off my mind. It's making me crazy. It was bad in the beginning, but it eased up once I decided to go back in the summer. Then in the last month, I haven't been able to do much other than think about her. And now that I want to reach out and let her know I want to see her, let her know how I feel, I can't get in touch with her!"

"I think you need some patience, lad. Things will work out." He stood up, and looked at his half-full glass of ouzo that he'd set on the table in front of him. "That shit is strong!"

"It is." I had to laugh. "I thought all you Irish guys could drink all day and night."

"We can!" He shook his head. "That's why I'm so confused by my reaction to the drink."

Clapping him on the back, I laughed some more. I'd never seen him so surprised before—and all by a simple drink. "I grew up on that stuff. I guess I've never realized just how potent it is."

"Guess not." Galen sat back down then looked at me with confusion. "I thought ya told me you had her number, Astor?"

I took a seat next to him and downed the glass of Scotch I'd poured myself. My strict diet hadn't gone entirely out the window, but I didn't seem to be able to make it through the days without a little alcohol now and then to numb my pain. "I did have her number and her parents' address in Miami." Rubbing my temples as I thought about how stupid I'd been, I went on, "I tossed it into the ocean not long after leaving the dock. And I've regretted doing that more times than I care to mention."

"That must've been hard." He looked at me with compassion in his eyes. "I don't believe in love, ya know. At least not for myself. But I think you might be in love with that girl, Astor. And I don't think that happens often for guys like us."

"It's never happened for me." I ran my hand over my face, feeling desperate. "I never thought she would stay in my heart, Galen. I swear I thought I would come back here and get lost in my work and barely think about her at all. That's why I didn't want her to leave the island with me; I thought I'd neglect her. I was so damn wrong. I miss her so much it hurts."

"Did ya tell her that ya loved her, Astor?" Galen put his hands behind his head and leaned back, settling into the sofa.

"Why would I have done that?" I knew I'd been wrong not to tell her how I felt. "I was leaving. I wouldn't even commit to letting her know I'd ever see her again. So what should I have been done? Tell her that I loved her and then left her anyway?"

Galen looked down at the floor. "I suppose you're right. I know we lead busy lives, you and I and others like us. We're not easy men to love. I can't see myself fallin' in love."

"I never saw me falling in love either. But it seems I have." I hadn't ever said anything like that out loud. "That sounds crazy coming out of my mouth."

With a nod, Galen agreed with me, "Yes, it does sound crazy. And you really need to analyze that. I mean, what would you do with Nova once you had her?" He eyed me with a knowing grin. "Would she be happy going with you all over the world? Or would you leave her here? With your family? And then how happy will Nova be? She has a job she loves and lives in a place that's as close to heaven as one can get."

"You're right." I looked away from him, not enjoying the reality check he'd just forced on me. I wasn't the same man I was on the island; I'd left that man behind. I was a businessman with tons of things I needed to tend to. Yet I'd been barely tending to anything. I'd been moping around like a lost puppy. "I'm glad you came by, Galen. I've been living in a dream world. I can't make Nova happy. I need to put her behind me."

"If you think that's what's best for her." Galen looked at me with a smile on his face. "We'll get busy in Spain. Our minds will be a million miles away from things like love. If you don't want to see Nova, if you want to keep her out of your mind, then stay away from Paradise. It's as easy as that. In no time at all, you'll get over her."

I hated that he was right. I've got to stop thinking about her and move on with my life.°

23

NOVA

W hen my two week vacation was over, I knew I had to go back to the island to talk to Camilla about the pregnancy. She'd eyed me suspiciously. "And you're sure it's not Astor's baby, Nova?"

"No. I was pregnant before I even came here; I just didn't realize it. It's a guy from back home in Miami. I've already told him. He's thrilled, and I'd like to have the baby in Miami. That means I'll need some extra time off, but I want to come back in the summer if that's okay. And would it be okay for the baby to go to the island daycare?"

"And what about the father?" Camilla asked. "We don't take on spouses here."

"No, we're not getting married. And he's got his own life to live anyway. I'll take the baby to see him when I have time off. He's cool with that." I couldn't believe how easily the lies were slipping off my tongue. But I knew she'd tell Astor about the pregnancy if she thought for one second the child was his.

A smile finally came over her face. "Well, congratulations, Momma. We can make accommodations for you and your little one. I'll set you up in the assistant manager's bungalow; it's more private than the rooms in staff housing. It's a two-bedroom unit just behind the lobby."

I found it odd she would put me in a place meant for another person. "And where will the assistant manager be staying? I don't want to put anyone out."

She pulled some papers out of her desk drawer. "Well, I wanted to surprise you with this, but since you've surprised me first, I guess I've got to just go ahead and tell you."

"Tell me what?" I had no clue what she was about to say.

"I'm giving you the assistant property manager job. But only if you want it." She pushed the contract toward me. "As you can see here, it means a substantial raise and the benefits increase as well. Your baby will get free daycare of course—and the new place, of course."

"I can't believe this." I felt like I might faint. "How? Why? When?" She'd rendered me speechless.

Camilla shook her head and laughed. "You're the perfect choice for this job, Nova. You're going to be taking college courses in the hospitality program. With this position, you can put your knowledge into practice. And Stacy quit, so you don't have to feel bad about taking anyone's place."

"She quit?" I asked.

"Yeah." Camilla got up and went to get a couple of bottles of water out of the fridge. "She didn't like being stuck out here. She felt trapped." She laughed. "Trapped in Paradise. Sounds like the title of a romance novel, doesn't it?"

"Kinda." I didn't know what else to say; my thoughts were stuck on how lucky I was, how great my life was turning out to be. "I appreciate this offer more than I can say. But will my taking time off when the baby comes affect my job?"

"Debbie can get along without you for a couple of months. You said the baby isn't due until February." She handed me a bottle of water. "You can see the resort's doctor for all your prenatal care, and he can report to your primary doctor back home. You can leave here in—let's say January? Or better yet, you can just stay home when you have Christmas vacation at the end of December. From there, you'll get paid medical leave until the first of May. How does that sound, Nova?"

"Like a miracle." I had not expected her to be so accommodating. "And I think you're the best boss in the entire world, Camilla. And I'm not just blowing smoke either. I really do think that!" I got up and went to throw my arms around her. "You've made things so much better for me. I promise you I'll never leave this place—or I'll never leave your employment. Not ever! Thank you so much!"

She patted my back. "It's okay, Nova. I know I've got a great employee in you. You made promoting you an easy choice. And I want to thank you for all your hard work. I know you'll be a part of this resort for a very long time, and I'll make sure your little family feels like this is home, too."

Now I just needed to make sure that she'd never tell Astor about the baby. I let her go and looked her in the eyes. "I'm going to need you to keep the baby information from anyone who might tell Astor. I don't want him throwing his weight around and making things diffi-cult for the baby's father and me. He can get very jealous when it comes to me. He might even demand a paternity test—and I know this baby isn't his, or I'd gladly have those tests done, Camilla. Can you understand where I'm coming from?"

She eyed me, not about to let me get by with lying to her. "How can you be so sure it's not his?"

"My last period was two months before I came to the island." That wasn't a lie. I'd just left out the fact that my monthlies had never been on time.

She walked away and took the seat behind her desk. "Okay, I see what you're saying. It couldn't be his. I'll keep this to myself. I mean, the staff will know, and I can't do anything about what any of them say. I'm sure it will be whispered about that Astor is the real father, but none of them have connections back to the man, so who cares, right?"

Relieved that she understood, I sat back down and started reading the contract. After signing it, Camilla showed me to my new office and I got settled in.

Lunchtime came around, and I walked over to The Royal to get something to eat. I heard footsteps behind me, and then Kyle stepped around me, pulling open the door to the restaurant. "Join me for lunch, Nova."

"Not even asking, just telling me, huh?" I knew what he wanted to talk about. "Sure, Kyle, I'd love to join you for lunch. How was your vacay?"

"Super, I went back to Seattle to see my family." He nodded at Donny, who jerked his head toward the dining room. "Take any table you'd like; there aren't any reservations today."

Kyle walked toward a table for two then pulled out a chair. "Madam."

I sat down and watched him take his seat. Kyle was a handsome guy. And I knew he was a Dom, too. I knew he'd try to use those domineering skills to get to the truth, so I just spilled everything. "I went to the doctor and found out I really am knocked up. Only thing is, I'm more knocked up than I realized. I was pregnant when I got here in May." I had to come up with a name for the fake father. My last boyfriend came to mind. "Dennis Fielding is the father. And he's really excited about the baby, too."

"Oh, yeah." He didn't believe a word I was saying, his stoic stare and deadpan eyes told me that—especially because he was the one who'd helped me come up with the lie. "So, when are you due, Nova?"

"February." I turned my attention to Petra, who came up to take our order. "Hey, girl."

"Hey, Nova. How was your vacation away from Paradise?" she asked.

I smiled at her. "Pretty great—in a weird way. I found out I'm pregnant."

Her eyes went wide. "And how does Astor feel about that?"

Kyle butted in. "Oh, it's not his, Petra. It's some dude named Dennis. Isn't that right, Nova?

Kyle wasn't sure about my story; I could see that in his eyes. "Hey, Petra, how about a couple of sodas and some cheeseburgers and fries for us this afternoon?"

She looked at me. "Is that okay with you, Nova?"

I saw that the Dom sitting across from me was doing what he did best—taking charge. "Nope. I'm going to do my best to eat healthy for this baby. I'd like a salad and a roasted chicken breast with brown rice and steamed broccoli. And no soda for me. I'll take water."

"Sure." Petra looked at Kyle disapprovingly. "I can see what you're doing, and I think it's kind of fucked up. She's pregnant. She doesn't need your kind of attention, if you know what I'm saying."

His eyes moved up to look at her. "Petra, my dear, you're in over your head with me. Get the food and don't worry about my business."

As she walked away, I had to ask, "So, who all knows about you, Kyle?"

"Petra knows a little. Not nearly as much as she could, though." He cocked one brow. "Three smacks to the ass and she was crying. I told her this wasn't for her, and that was the end of it. And just to make sure you know what I'm doing here with you...I'm not trying to make you mine, Nova. I'm merely watching out for a fellow Dom's Sub. A Sub who might be keeping a secret from her Dom that she shouldn't be. One that might get her tight little ass strung up and whipped for being disobedient, conniving, and dishonest."

"I'm not Astor's Sub anymore. That contract is over." I knew Astor would never do those kinds of things to me anyway. "And he's not like that."

"Let him find out you had his baby without telling him, and watch that Dom in him come out, guns blazing." He laughed. "Are you really that naïve, Nova? He's going to want to wring your neck when he finds out what you're doing. Keeping his kid away from him? I know we talked about this when you took the pregnancy test, but I think this is a bad idea. Keeping it a secret from him? He's going to lose his fucking mind, and in the process, you will be punished more severely than you can even imagine. They make dungeons for naughty little Subs like you, honey. Do yourself a favor and tell Camilla to let the man know he's having a baby."

He had me shaking, I had to admit that. But then I knew Astor, and Kyle didn't. "Well, I'm not worried at all. This baby isn't his. He'd have no right to be angry for not telling him. And I've told you already, he doesn't want a baby. He doesn't have time for a family. The only that telling him would accomplish is making him angry. He's really jealous about me, and knowing he and I were screwing while I carried another man's baby would probably make him physically ill. Why would I want to make the man I love feel that way?"

"Tell me why you love that man and yet you're going to have another guy's baby." Kyle smiled at me as if he'd won the argument.

"I have no choice. I'm not getting rid of this baby. I love it already." I shook my head; he just didn't understand.

He threw his head back, laughing. "Nova, I can see right through you. Your Dom will too. And he'll come back next summer, I can tell you that right now. And when he does, he'll know the truth without you having to say a thing to him."

Maybe I can't stay here.

24

ASTOR

T he middle of April had me thinking full-time about Nova and going back to the island. I knew she'd be back in May. I knew that I could take time off.

Galen and I had decided to go through with the Spain project, but I didn't have to be there to get things done. I could do whatever I wanted, and all I wanted was to see Nova.

As hard as Galen kept trying to help me get my mind off the woman, he failed every time. And he admitted that he'd been drunk each time he went on his little spiel questioning whether Nova would ever fit into my life. He'd told me that I had been right, that I should go back to the island and make things real with the woman who'd stolen my heart.

Fingering the ring I had in my pocket, I wondered if Nova really had waited for me. If she had, then I had an important question to ask her. If she hadn't, then I'd already have my answer, and I would leave her alone.

No woman had turned my head even once in the months we'd been apart. I knew no one ever would. Not as long as Nova had my heart. And she would hold it in her hands until she said she didn't want me.

I could admit now that I'd been more worried about her not wanting anything to do with me than I'd ever been worried about anything else. If the pain had been too great for her to bear alone, she might've looked for comfort in another man's arms.

If she'd done that, I couldn't take it. The thought of anyone else touching what was mine made me so angry it scared me. Although the contract had long been over, in my mind, I still belonged to that girl. I prayed she felt the same.

Picking up the phone, I finally called Galen to tell him I would be going to the island on the first of May. "Galen, I hope you're doing well."

"I am. How are ya, my friend?" he asked.

"I'm doing well, too. I wanted to tell you that I'd like to come to Paradise for the summer." I hesitated to say the rest.

"Of course," he said right away.

I had more to say, 'I would very much like it if no one else was told about my visit. I'd like to surprise Nova."

"You sure that's a good idea?" he asked.

"No." I laughed. "But I want to do it anyway."

I knew he'd do what I'd asked. "Well, then no one will know. I'll let you stay with me in my bungalow; there's tons of room. I'm sure you hope to be stayin' at your girl's place anyway."

"Can I stay in her room?" I had no idea it that would even be an option.

"Oh, yeah. I forgot that I've never told ya the news," he said. "But then again, I just got it myself a few days ago."

"The news?" I asked, feeling a bit tense for some reason. "Tell me, Galen."

"Camilla gave Nova a new job," he said.

"What kind of new job?"

Galen chuckled. "A great one. She's been made the assistant manager, and that comes with a two-bedroom bungalow. So you could stay with her if she'll have ya."

"You guys have already moved her up?" I asked. "In only a year's time?"

"Camilla has. I had nothing to do with that," Galen informed me. "She's the boss over there. I leave it all up to her—and she's crazy about Nova. I think she's got plans for the girl."

"So her future is there then," I said, mostly to myself.

"I know I was tipsy when I told ya she might be better off right where she is. But I'm sober now, and I still think that way. Leave her working where she's happiest. You can come and go as you please, do what you want or need to do; you could still make it work. But give her a firm foundation to live on, Astor. Taking her off to Greece might not be the best thing for you two."

He was right and I knew that. "I'll figure things out. I've got to. She told me before that a lot of people make long-distance relationships work. If others can do it, so can we. If she'll still have me, that is."

"I'm sure she will." He hesitated, leaving a gap filled with silence. "But if she won't, then let her be. My mother told me once that if you love someone, you've got to let them go. You can't hold them too tightly, or you'll smother them. It sounds like good advice, even if I've never had to apply it myself."

"It does." I didn't want to think about letting Nova go again. "Well, I'll see you on May first then, Galen. Mum's the word now."

"Yes, I'll remember. Goodbye, friend."

The end of our call left me feeling strange. My heart pounded, my head felt light, and I took a seat near the fountain outside of my home. My mother spotted me from across the way and came to sit next to me. "So, you're going to see that woman, huh?"

Mom wasn't real happy about me being with an American. "Yes, I'm going to go back to the island to see her. And just so you know, I may not be coming back here much after that. If she'll have me, I'm going to make that place my home."

Her eyes filled with tears. "We barely see you as it is, Astor. Can't you bring her here? We'll be good to her. I promise you, we will."

Wrapping my arm around her shoulders, I hugged her. "I don't want to bring her here and leave her. She's got a career that she loves. She's going to college to climb the ladder; she's already started climbing. I don't want to stop her. Bringing her here—expecting her to live here—that would stop her."

Sniffling, she pulled a tissue out of her bra then blew her nose. "I see what you're saying. But I miss seeing you as it is. I hope you can bring her and come home to visit. If you're going to settle down, then why not do it here?"

"I'm not sure how much settling I'll be doing. I want to keep working the way I have been, just not quite as much. And when I'm in between projects, I want to spend my time with her." I kissed my mother's cheek. "But I will bring her to visit as often as possible." I hated to see her sad. "I promise."

"You better keep that promise, son." She took my face between her meaty hands. "I mean it. And if you two get married, you better let us throw the wedding, Astor Christakos. You know I live for that kind of thing."

"I do," I said with a laugh. "And if she agrees, then we will have the wedding here. But let's not get ahead of ourselves. I haven't spoken to her since I left the island months ago. And when I left, I made it clear to her that I might never see her again. She may have moved on."

My mother grinned at me. "No, she would never move on. Not from my boy, she wouldn't. Only a fool would move on from you, Astor." She kissed my cheek. "When you ask her to marry you, and she says yes, bring her to meet us. I want to welcome her to our family with open arms."

I wished I'd had the same confidence my mother had that Nova hadn't moved on, and I wished like hell that I didn't have this ache in my heart.

I'd never been the kind of man who mooned over a woman. And I didn't like the feeling it gave me.

One thing I knew was that seeing Nova again would end this. Either I would give in to love and sink into its depths, or I would know for certain it doesn't exist, and I'd be able to move on.

Nova held all the cards. She alone held my heart in her hands. What she would do with it was anybody's guess.

I'd planned on owning her, but it turned out that she owned me —heart and all. Not in a million years did I see this coming.

Leaving my mother, I headed to my quarters to be alone. It was hard being around people while my head was such a mess. I hoped that if Nova would have me, then I could get back to being myself. I knew I would never be the same as I'd been before I'd visited Paradise, but I wouldn't feel so worried and lonely all the time, missing her. If those feelings were gone, then I could focus on so much more.

One way or the other, I would make a change in my life. Go back to the old me and never look back, or move on to a new me and never look back. Either way, I wasn't ever going to look back.

Lying on my bed, I closed my eyes, picturing Nova as I so often did these days: her naked body lying on the bed next to me; her hands moving over her luscious tits while her hazel eyes gazed back at me.

My cock swelled just thinking about her that way. "You're beautiful," I'd whisper.

She'd smile. "So are you."

Easing down, I would take her soft, sweet lips with a gentle kiss. My hand would run through her silky hair as she parted her lips, inviting me in. Our kiss would grow as I caressed her creamy skin.

Arching up, she would silently beg me for more. I would know the moment she couldn't go on without feeling me inside of her. And I would need to be inside of her, too. That's the only place where either of us would feel whole.

Two parts of the same spirit, we would become one once more. No time or space could separate what we'd created with our bond. I knew I could be halfway around the world and hear her voice, and that alone would be enough to take me back to her—to the two of us, alone in our room, making love, sharing ourselves in a way that only those who love each other can.

I belonged with her. She belonged with me. No one could ever come between us. No one. Nothing. It would be she and I forever and ever.

The orgasm took me by surprise, bringing me out of my fantasy. Gasping for breath as I looked down at the mess I'd made, I closed my eyes so I didn't have to see it.

Had I made a mess out of things? Had I ruined what could've been the most authentic love that I could ever be a part of? Had I walked away when I should've stayed?

So many months had passed and not a word said between us. Not one instance of contact, even through a third party, had been made.

I'd left my number with the woman who'd answered Galen's call, but I'd never received a call from Nova.

Had she gotten my message but hadn't wanted to call me?

Maybe I shouldn't go back to the island after all.

25

NOVA

S tepping off the boat with three-month-old Mia in my arms, I inhaled the salty air and sighed, "We're home, honey."

It was early in the morning, and no one was up and moving around as I took my daughter to our home. The porter brought our things to the bungalow behind the lobby. "This is a nice place, Nova. It's good to have you back," Jack said as he brought my things inside.

"Thank you. It's good to be back." I waved goodbye to him as I took my baby girl to see her new home. I walked into my bedroom and saw a bassinet next to my bed. A pink ribbon stuck to the top held a card attached—it was a gift from Petra.

I'd told everyone that the baby would be a girl before leaving to deliver her, and Camilla had told me that they would have a baby shower without me while I was back in Miami. She'd had all the things brought to my home and put away nicely.

Going to the next room, I found a gorgeous baby crib and a closet full of clothes. "Oh my God!" I hugged Mia and nearly cried when I saw all the beautiful things everyone had gotten for her. "Seems you're going to be well-loved here in Paradise, Mia."

This baby would never go without. And I knew we were in the

right place. I'd thought and thought about whether coming back to work here was the smartest thing to do. But in the end, I knew I would never get a better opportunity than I had in Paradise.

A knock at the door had me going back to the living room where Camilla stood. "Give her here." She held her arms out, wiggling her fingers. "I've been dying to hold her."

Handing her over, I had to kiss Mia on the forehead before giving her away. "It's so good to be back here. My parents are great, but man, do they hover. Finally, I'll get to be the mom I want to be, instead of trying to follow every piece of *helpful* advice my parents are always giving me."

"She's so cute," Camilla gushed. "Who's a pretty girl? You are." She cooed before looking at me briefly. "I'm so going to obsess over this child—just saying."

"You should have one, too. That way she'll have someone to play with." I winked before walking away to unpack things while I had someone to look after the baby. "What time are the guests going to begin arriving today?"

"Noon." Camilla cooed at Mia before going on. "And you're expected to be there, too. All the staff, as you know. Mia can stay in the daycare with Angie and Marla while you do that. After that, you can have her in your office as much as you want to."

"I can?" I had to smile. "I was going to ask you about that."

Camilla came to lean on my doorframe, still holding Mia, who gazed at her with the typical fascination of a newborn. "Of course, you can have her there as much as you want. Just take her to the girls when you need to or want to. So how did the delivery go?"

"Painfully." I laughed. "At first, anyway. Once they gave me the epidural, I was fine." I couldn't admit to her that I had been kind of sad and even cried when Mia was first put into my arms—not only because she was a gorgeous little miracle, but also because Astor wasn't there to see our miracle.

"And how did Daddy like the birthing process?" she asked.

I'd forgotten about the fake dad. "Oh, he was cool with it. He's a real laid-back guy."

"Must be pretty chill if he doesn't care that he can't see his kid all summer long." She looked at me with knowing eyes. "Are you sure you want to stick with your story, Nova? This little girl has the bluest eyes I've ever seen, but that green tint to them isn't something you see very often."

She had her father's eyes. I couldn't hide that fact. She also had his dark hair, another thing I couldn't hide. "Look, Astor told me flat out that he didn't want kids. He doesn't have time for a girlfriend or a kid. I'm trying to avoid ruining his life, Camilla. And that's exactly what I would be doing if I told him about her."

Camilla smiled at Mia, and my baby smiled right back as she reached out to touch Camilla's cheek. "You wouldn't ruin anyone's life, would you, my precious little baby girl?"

I pulled my uniform out of the closet and held it up to me as I stood in front of the mirror. "Looks like it'll still fit. I'm a few pounds over my pre-pregnancy weight. But I don't think that'll show."

"I don't even see any difference in your weight. I'm sure you'll be okay." Camilla watched me as I crossed the room. "So, since you've told me the truth, tell me how the delivery really was?"

"Bittersweet." I brushed my hair then put it into a bun. "I missed him so much during the last few months. And when I went to the hospital, I just kept thinking how great he would be at keeping my mind off the pain." I looked at myself in the mirror. "And I've missed him every single day since she was born. And every single day before that." Suddenly it occurred to me that he might be coming back to the island today. "Is he scheduled to arrive today?" I asked, slightly panicked at the thought.

She shook her head. "Nope. I guess he's not coming. Maybe you're right. Maybe he's just way too busy to handle a girlfriend. If he's too busy for that, then he's too busy for a baby, I'd expect." She kissed Mia on the forehead again. "You're giving me baby-fever, Mia."

"Have one, come on!" I urged her. "I don't want to be the only mom who works here. You're married. Tell the hubby it's time to start procreating."

"I just might do that." She sat on the bed. "Is she always this good?"

"So far." I took off the dress I had on to put on the khaki shorts and white button-down. "The first week was pure hell. Getting up every two hours to feed her. After that week, she and I both calmed down, and things have been going smoothly ever since. I fell in love with her before she was ever born, but once I saw her face, she stole my heart for good."

Camilla watched the way Mia looked at me as I crossed the floor, walking near her. "Seems you've stolen her heart, too, Mommy."

"Hope so." I slipped on my sandals and ran my hands down my sides. "I'm back."

"Yes, you are." Camilla laughed. "And it's so good to have you back —and your little bundle of joy! This is going to be a great year. I can already tell."

I had high hopes it would be. Only one thing worried me. "Now that you know about Astor being her father, do you think you can help me with Kyle? He knows the truth, too, and he's kind of been a jackass about telling Astor."

Nodding, she said, "Doms do tend to stick together."

"I think, for now, that I can keep her away from him. I just won't take her out much. The daycare is only a short walk from here. If I can make sure he's not around, he won't see her." I knew it was a stretch but didn't know what else to do.

"I'll handle Kyle." She looked at me then winked. "I am his boss. If he wants to keep his job here, he'll mind his own damn business."

"I knew I liked you." I smiled and sat on the bed next to her and ran my fingers over Mia's little head. "Every time I look at her, I think of Astor. She's going to be the most beautiful girl on the planet. Of course, I am her mother, so I might be a little biased."

"No, she's going to be gorgeous." Camilla let the baby hold her pinky finger. "Wait, going to be? No. She's gorgeous now. She'll just get better as time goes on."

Camilla couldn't take the smile off her face. "She does have her daddy's great looks. Let's just pray she doesn't have his demeanor."

I couldn't help but laugh. "Oh, we're awful, aren't we?"

"Yes," she agreed. "Come on! Let's go eat breakfast and let everyone meet her. And don't even think about worrying about Kyle. I'll set him straight right away. He won't say a word."

Happy with having the boss on my side, I grabbed the diaper bag and away we went on our first island outing.

For the longest time that morning, Kyle didn't even show up to eat at Toucan's, the best breakfast restaurant the island offered. But when he did, he made a B-line for Mia who was being held by Alexis. "And who do we have here?" he asked.

I tensed up, but Camilla placed her hand on my shoulder. "Let me." She made her way across the room and stood right next to Kyle, who eyed my daughter. "Isn't she precious, Kyle?"

"Oh, yeah." He ran his finger over her cheek. "And would you look at those eyes?" He looked up at Camilla. "Remind you of anyone?"

The way she simply smiled at Kyle made me smile, too. "No. She doesn't. You like your job here, right, Kyle?"

He blinked a few times before answering, "Yes, ma'am, I do."

"That's good." She put her hand on his shoulder. "Come with me. I want to talk about your duties as a host, Kyle."

I knew he was no longer a threat, and that took a load off my shoulders. The others might think Mia looked a lot like Astor, but none of them cared enough to seek him out to tell him anything if they had the opportunity.

For now, I felt safe.

When noon came around, I took Mia to stay with the ladies at the daycare while I went to greet the guests. Astor wasn't on the list, so I knew I didn't have anything to worry about.

Mr. Dunne's yacht was the first to arrive. I figured he'd get there first since he liked to greet his guests personally. We all stood still, hands behind our back, waiting for our boss to come out of the cabin to say hello.

He emerged and stepped off the boat and onto the dock. "Happy to see you all!" He took a bow. "I want to thank you for all of your hard work this past year. I'm lookin' forward to many, many more years to come."

"Aye, aye," we all shouted.

The luggage came up and porters took it all away. There seemed to be so much of it—twice the usual amount. But who knew what he'd brought to the island? It wasn't for me to question.

I turned my attention to the other yacht that was approaching in the distance before looking back at Galen's still tied to the dock. It would need to move, so the other could dock.

The cabin door opened and a tall figure stepped out. The dark glasses and baseball cap could not hide the identity of the man standing just feet away from me.

Astor!

26

ASTOR

I couldn't recall a time I'd been so apprehensive. It took every ounce of courage I had to walk out of the yacht's cabin and onto the deck. Nova was out there waiting, but not for me.

She'd had no idea I'd be stepping off Galen's boat that day. No idea I was coming back for her—for good, this time. And I had no idea if she still wanted me. No idea if she'd moved on or not.

Putting my sunglasses on, I pulled the baseball cap down, trying to disguise myself a bit. I'd worn shorts and a T-shirt to give myself a casual appearance. I wanted Nova to witness the change she'd made in me. I was no longer the man who thought only about work, no longer the man who didn't care about other people's feelings. Nova had worn off on me. Her caring attitude had overridden my indifference.

My heart thumped hard in my chest as I looked at the line of people on one side of the dock. Scanning them all, I found Nova with a tightly clenched jaw, staring straight at me.

In my dreams, she'd broken into a run, coming to me with her arms wide, shouting my name over and over. And in those dreams, she'd always worn a smile. She wasn't smiling at me now. Real life didn't seem to be anything like my dreams.

Gulping, I strode ahead, my eyes on Nova and only on her. Happy or not, she was there, and I knew I had to win her back if I had in fact lost her. I had to have her. I knew it with every fiber of my being that I had to make her mine again—this time I would never let her go.

She looked up at me as I came to a stop in front of her. "Glad to see me?"

"You weren't on the guest list," her voice broke on the last word. "I didn't know you were coming." She looked down, and I saw her body shaking. "You never called."

"Neither did you." Nothing was going as I thought it would. This wasn't how I'd wanted our reunion to be.

Jerking her head back up, she glared at me. "You didn't give me your number, Astor. How was I to call you?"

"Shit!" the woman next to her hissed. She looked at Nova. "I forgot all about it. Mr. Dunne called me earlier this year. He'd been asking about you. You changed your number, remember?"

Nova looked confused. "Yes, I remember changing my number. What does Mr. Dunne have to do with this, Debbie?"

Debbie looked apologetic as she said, "He gave me Mr. Christakos's phone number, and I was supposed to give it to you and tell you to call him. I forgot all about it—I'm so sorry."

I took Nova by the chin to make her look at me. "We called in January. You've had access to me since then. It's not my fault you didn't get the message. I wanted to speak with you."

"You had my number though," she countered.

With a sigh, I made my confession, "I threw it away when you didn't show up to tell me goodbye. I was hurt. It was a stupid thing to do, and I've regretted it the whole time we were apart." I looked at the line of people, many of whom were looking at us. "Can we go somewhere and talk, Nova?"

"I'm afraid not. It's my job to greet all the guests, Astor. Maybe we can talk after my duties are done. We'll see." She shifted her weight, and it was only then that I noticed her hands were still clasped behind her back.

I opened my arms. "A hug before I have to leave you?"

She held her breath, her chest full and still. Then she opened her arms and moved into mine. "I have missed you."

The sweet scent of coconut and lime wafted up to me, and I breathed her in. Her body felt perfect in my arms. I almost felt whole again. *Almost.*

"I've missed you more than you will ever understand, Nova." I kissed the top of her head and felt butterflies in my stomach for the first time in forever. "I hope we can get back to where we were before I left."

She pulled her body out of my arms and wiped the tears that had escaped from her eyes with the back of her hand. "We'll talk later, Astor. Please. I don't want to do this with everyone watching us," she whispered.

"Me, neither." I looked at the woman next to her and asked, "Debbie, since you've made such a huge mistake by not giving Nova my number five months ago, do you think it would be alright if she didn't have to stand here and greet the rest of the guests? She and I need to talk."

Nova shook her head. "No, Astor. That's not fair to the others. I will see you later."

I couldn't believe she'd dismissed me that way. "Fine." I turned to leave and felt the heat of her gaze on me.

"I'll come to see you later, Astor. I'm sorry," came her apology.

At least she'd given one. I just kept walking, mad at her and myself.

As I walked into Galen's bungalow, he grinned at me. "So, how did it go with Nova? Was she glad to see ya?"

"Not really." I flopped on the sofa and jerked my head toward the kitchen. "Do you have anything to drink in there?"

Galen walked to the kitchen then came back with two beers. "Here ya go." He took a seat across from me. "So what the hell happened, Astor?"

"She's mad at me. I told her about giving that Debbie woman my number in January, and that didn't seem to make much difference to her." I took a drink of the beer. "I've never felt like this, Galen. It's uncomfortable as hell." I took another drink. "What the hell am I supposed to do now?"

"How the hell should I know?" He laughed then took a drink of his beer. "Let's just get drunk and see where that takes us."

I was on board with that. I downed the beer then got up to get another one. "Women are the most incomprehensible creatures on the planet. How can Nova be so damn sweet and hospitable, yet so cold and mean?"

"I'm sure she'll thaw out. She's just mad about you not calling. I'm sure that's it." Galen leaned back, relaxing in a way I envied. "You've got three months to get her back. I have faith in ya, lad."

"I don't want it to take three damn months to get her back. I want her back right now." I opened the new beer and chugged most of that one, too. "Damn it!"

Just as I was about to drink the other half, there was a knock at the door. "Astor?"

I slammed the bottle down on the counter then sprinted to the door. "Nova!"

Galen got up, heading to his bedroom. "I'll leave you two alone."

I opened the door and didn't hesitate, scooping her up and bringing her inside. "Baby, you're here sooner than I thought you'd be."

My lips crashed down on hers, but her hands pressed against my chest, pushing me back. "Astor, no."

My breath ragged, it sounded like I'd just run a hundred miles. "Why not?"

"Astor, I can't do this." She shook her head. "Put me down. We need to talk."

I put her feet on the floor and turned back to the kitchen. "I think I'll need my beer for this." My hands shook as I picked the bottle back up and downed the rest. I reached into the fridge to grab another. "Want one?"

"No, thank you." She took a seat in the chair, making sure I couldn't sit next to her. "I don't drink alcohol."

"You gave it up, huh?" I opened the beer. "I took up drinking. It's helped dull the pain."

"What pain?" she asked with furrowed brows.

I sat on the sofa and leaned back. "The pain of losing you, Nova. I've been a shell of my former self ever since I left this island and you. I haven't been able to do much of anything, other than think about you. But it seems you haven't had the same problem." I took a drink. "I thought you would be happy about me coming back, but you seem kind of pissed about it."

"I'm not mad." She looked at the ceiling. "Just surprised. If I had known you were coming, I think I would've prepared myself for this."

"Why would you need to prepare yourself to see me, Nova?" I put the beer down on the coffee table in front of me. It suddenly felt like I needed to have all my wits about me; this was turning into an important conversation. "Better yet, why didn't you come to say goodbye to me that day?"

Now she was put on the spot, and it showed in her pained expression. "Astor, I meant to go back to be with you until the boat came. I really did. But something came up, and I couldn't be there. I didn't mean to hurt you."

I could not believe what she'd said. "Something came up? What the fuck could've been so important that you would leave me wondering what happened? I tossed your number because I thought you might've been lying to me the whole time about how you felt about me. It's been killing me, wondering if you only treated me the way you did because you felt it was your job to do so."

Shaking her head, frowning, she said, "No. That had nothing to do with it. The truth is I fell in love with you, Astor. And it was tearing me apart that you didn't love me back."

"I did love you, Nova." I thought better about what I'd said. "No. I meant to say that I *do* love you. Baby, I love you more than I ever believed I could love anyone."

She sat there, wringing her hands in her lap, holding her jaw so tightly it looked like it hurt. "Astor, why did you come back?"

"For you." My head ached so badly it felt as if it would blow up if she didn't stop fighting this. "I want you, Nova. I came back here for you and only you. Can you just accept my apology, and we can get back to where we were?"

"I accept your apology if that helps you at all." She sighed. "But you need to know that I've changed a lot. I'm not the woman you left behind, Astor. I'm different now."

"I can see that." I looked at her. "You certainly have a lot more hostility than I remember. And you're lacking that empathy you had so much of, too."

"I've been hurt." She shrugged her shoulders. "I've never been hurt the way you hurt me. It changes a person. Besides, how would things be if I just let us go back to where we were before you left?"

It sounded like she might be thinking about giving me a shot. "I would write up a new contract, only this one wouldn't have an end date."

Her hazel eyes scanned my body, and I felt heat build inside of me. "And you think that's something I would want?"

Didn't see that coming.

"I did think that. Am I wrong?" My gut began to twist as she gave me a stoic expression.

She stood and looked down at me. "I won't be signing any Dom/Sub contract with you again, Astor. If that's all you want—a sex slave—then count me out."

She walked past me, and I caught her hand, stopping her hasty retreat. "That's not all I want, Nova. Not by a long-shot."

Her eyes were glued to where I held her hand. "I've gotta go. Let me go, please."

"Nova, don't leave. Please." I couldn't believe it'd come to this so quickly—begging.

This was not at all the romantic welcome I was hoping for. But I wasn't willing to give up on her just yet.

27

NOVA

Astor's hand held mine, sending a shock of electricity through me. I needed to leave. Anger bubbled below the surface; I was mad about so many things.

Mad that he had surprised me like this, taking me off guard. Mad that Debbie hadn't given me the message when I called to give her my new number at the end of January. Mad that my body was betraying me so badly with pure need for him.

Astor could've been with me for the delivery of our baby if she'd given me that number.

If I'd have told him about the pregnancy, that is. I didn't know if I would've done that or not. As it was, I was still on the fence about it, but I knew I'd have to and soon.

All of the staff knew I'd come back with a baby, and it wouldn't be long before Astor heard about that, too. Worse, I'd already overheard a few of the girls remarking on how much Mia resembled Astor, though none had said a word about it to my face.

"You should leave, Astor," the words came out of my mouth before I realized what I was saying.

His expression told me I'd hurt him. "You don't want me here?"

He let go of my hand and looked down as I tried to explain.

"Look, it's just that I don't think you're going to have a good time here. I can't do this with you anymore. I can't be with you the way you want. You're still Astor Christakos, busy businessman, right? You're still going to need to leave when summer is over and get back to work, right?

And I'll be here. I'm not leaving this place, Astor. I'm not going to go sit in some mansion in Greece waiting around for you to stop by once in a while in between projects. I don't know if that's what you had in mind or what, but you should know that's not what I want."

"Have you found another man, Nova?" He looked up at me with droopy eyes. I'd never seen him look so hurt.

It made me feel terrible. "No, I haven't found another man, Astor. That's not why I'm saying this. I just can't devote my time to you the way I did last summer."

I had a baby to take care of now. And I also had to figure out how to handle telling him about that. I'd never thought he'd actually show up. I hadn't prepared what I would do in this situation.

He patted his lap. "Come, sit down. Let me stroke your hair and hold you and you'll fall back in love with me. I just need to touch you, Nova. I know you've got a different job now, and that means you can't be with me as much as you were last summer. But we can spend the nights together. We can still find time to be together. I could stay in your bungalow with you. Galen told me you have a two bedroom all to yourself now."

Not exactly all to myself. I had the baby there, too. "So, you thought you'd just show up, and I'd invite you to stay with me? And things would go right back to the way they were last year."

He nodded. "Yeah, I was hoping. Why can't it be that way? I'm sorry about throwing your number away, but now you know that I tried to get in contact with you. I should've done that a lot sooner, I can see that now. But the reason I didn't do it sooner was because I didn't know if you wanted me anymore. I was still too hurt to make that move before January. You haven't moved on, and I still want you. I don't see why you and I can't put this behind us and move forward."

He had no idea how badly I wanted to jump into his lap, snuggle into his broad chest, and just go back to how it was before. But that wasn't an option now. "Forward? Another summer fling? That's all this would be, Astor. Just three more months of sex, then you'd be gone again, leaving me high and dry. No, thank you."

"First of all, you're talking like that wasn't the best sex you've ever had. And three more months of that wouldn't bother you a bit." He gave me a brief, cocky grin before his expression became serious once again. "There's something more going on, Nova. Something you're not telling me."

God, he's good!

"Well, what I am telling you is that I can't go back to the way we were. I can't take three months of being with you, falling back in love with you, and then have you leave me again. I just won't allow myself to go through that again." I folded my arms and stomped one foot to make my point.

He smiled. "Maybe it wouldn't have to be just three months. What if I stayed longer than that?"

"How can you stay longer than that? I thought you were a very busy man." I deepened my voice, doing my best imitation of Astor. "I thought you didn't have time for anyone in your life. That's what you said all last summer. What's happened since then to change that?"

He laughed and threw his hands up. "I fell in love. That's what happened to change things."

It felt good to hear him say those words, but it killed me that I couldn't say them back to him. I had a child now. And she didn't deserve to have a father who flitted in and out of her life. She deserved a full-time father—just as much as I deserved a full-time partner. Astor couldn't be that for her, and I knew that.

What I still didn't know was how the hell I should go about telling him that I'd had a baby. I'd never been in such a tight spot in my life. "Astor, you really should get back on that yacht and leave this island. It would be the best thing for all of us if you did that."

"All of us?" he asked with a confused expression. "Who is all of us, Nova? There's just you and me. And how would my leaving help us get back together? I know I made a huge mistake, leaving you. I know

I've hurt you. And I know that I'm not going anywhere. I'll do everything in my power to get you back. You might as well get used to seeing me, baby. I'm not going anywhere.

"I know you still love me. You're hurt, but that'll go away with time. It'll go away a hell of a lot faster if you stop fighting this and just let it happen. We could go to your place, climb into your bed and all that hurt will disappear. I've got a fair amount of pain myself that needs to be washed away. And only your love will do that for me. The same way my love will do it for you."

Oh, that sounds a perfect way to spend the day.

But I couldn't do that, no matter how much he and I both wanted it. "Astor, you shouldn't waste your time on me." My heart hurt just saying those words. "I want more than you can give me." Truer words had never been spoken. I needed him to be a father, and I knew he couldn't be that. "You might be able to give me more of your time than you previously thought. But I'll need more than you have to give."

"And how do you know that?" He leaned forward to pick up his beer. "Are you sure you don't want a drink? I can tell you're tense. I'm sure a year without sex is playing a big part in that. I know, because I've been celibate for that long, too, and I know I could use an icebreaker. It would be a lot better than using alcohol to do it." His voice had gone seductive, and his abrupt, honest statements reminded me so much of the time we'd spent together last summer.

Watching him take a long drink of that cold beer made my mouth water. Thinking about having sex with him again had my juices flowing like a river.

Just one time, come on.

"I'm not hopping into bed with you, Astor." I wanted to. Oh, man did I want to. But I had Mia to think about now. Plus, my tits would leak all over the man, and that would be a dead giveaway that I'd had a baby while we'd been apart. I could feel my boobs filling with milk right then. "I've gotta go. I've got work to do." I really had to go pump before they started shooting milk out on their own.

I hurried toward the door and nearly exploded when I felt his hard body behind mine, pinning me up against the door. His breath was hot on my neck.

"Stop." His hands moved up and down my sides, making my thighs shake with desire, with craving him between them. His lips pressed against my neck. "I'm sorry. I will say those words to you a million times if that will make you believe me." He kissed a line along my shoulder. "I love you, Nova. I'm going to make things work for us. Give me a chance, baby. That's all I'm asking for—a chance to show you that I can make things work for us."

But can he make things work for a baby, too?

Every part of me wanted him. My body was on fire, and my sex throbbed with need. But I couldn't give in. He would find out my secret, and I couldn't have that. I needed to figure out how to keep it a secret from him for however long it took for him to get tired of chasing me and leave the island.

"Astor, please," I begged him as he grazed my skin with his lips.

"Nova, please," he whispered. "Please forgive me and come back to me. That's all I want: you, back in my life. I don't need anyone but you. Please, baby."

I felt drunk, my head light, my body weak. The hot pressure of his body on mine intoxicated me. Hearing him say words I'd dreamed of hearing from his lips countless times was too much. The way his mouth moved over my neck took all my will away. I turned around, and his mouth sought mine with a hard kiss.

My hands moved up his arms, taking in the muscles I'd longed to touch again. He lifted me, and I ran my legs around his waist as he pushed me against the door. His cock bulged against my cunt, grinding into me. I moved my hands under his T-shirt to feel his muscular back. Its hills and valleys were so familiar to me.

He moved his mouth off mine to kiss my neck, nibbling it as he whispered, "I love you, Nova. Let me prove it to you, baby."

I tangled my hands in his soft dark waves. "Astor, please understand that I'm not doing this to hurt you. It's just that I can't," I had to say the words out loud, to remind myself as well. I inhaled sharply as he bit down on my neck hard, making me soak my panties. It felt so damn good. "Oh, God! Astor, please."

He sucked at the spot he'd bitten, then whispered, "Don't say you can't. You can. You will. You are mine. You always have been, and you always will be. Stop fighting me. Give me what I want. You know you want this, too."

If I had only myself to consider, then I would've given in to the man. He was right—I did want him. But there was a child to think about now. And she needed me more than I needed Astor. There was only one thing to do.

Lowering myself to the ground, I put my hand behind me, turned the doorknob and pulled myself away from the man who'd turned me to jelly. "I can't. I'm sorry." And then I ran like the wind.

28

ASTOR

W ith my cock throbbing, I stood in the doorway, watching Nova haul ass away from me. "What the hell just happened?"

Galen cleared his throat as he came back into the living room. "I think you've got quite a problem on your hands there." He strolled over to the fridge and got himself another beer.

I went to the bathroom, too stunned to say anything. My cock hurt, my heart hurt, my head hurt—everything fucking hurt. All I could do was stare in the mirror and ask myself, "Why? What more could you have done, Astor Christakos?"

After washing my face and waiting for my erection go down, I went back to sit down with Galen and hash out where I'd gone wrong. He looked at me with a frown on his face. "Maybe you were wrong for coming here without letting her know first, Astor. Maybe it's the shock of suddenly seeing you that has her all riled up."

Nodding, I picked up my beer again. "Maybe. But damn it, why should that stop us from being together? So I made a mistake by just showing up. So what?"

"I suppose women take longer to get over these things than men do." He took a drink and picked up one of the menus off the coffee table. "Let's order lunch in. You don't seem to be in good enough spirits to go out in public yet."

"Yeah, I'm not leaving this bungalow until I figure out what I need to do to get Nova back." I got up to throw away the now empty beer bottle and see if there was anything a bit stronger to drink. "I want a steak from The Royal. Tell them it's for me, and the chef will know how to cook it. I need some protein to help me deal with this woman. I don't know what's gotten into me. I thought I had her there for a second, but then she bolted."

"I'm getting lobster," he called out to me. "You want a lobster tail with your steak, Astor?"

"No. Just the steak. And some salad, too. Maybe some steamed broccoli. And get them to bring something some more alcohol, too— something strong. I'm going to need a lot of that." I looked through the cabinets, not finding anything that I could use to drown my sorrows.

Galen placed the order as I sat back down with a beer in my hand. He hung up the phone and looked at the beer. "You should slow down. I've never seen you drink so much."

"I've never needed to drink this much." I put the beer down on the table so I wouldn't be tempted to down it. "I thought love was supposed to be a good thing. How can something that's supposed to be so amazing make me feel this way? I don't understand it."

"I just hope this never happens to me." He laughed, but I frowned. "Sorry. But I do hope that."

"I hope this never happens to you, either," I had to admit. "I just know that if she came around, then my life would be better than I can even imagine. At least that's what I'm hoping for. That's what I'm sticking around to find out, anyway. I feel like I'm so close to having that.

"My thoughts on what her initial reaction to seeing me would be were way off, though. I hope I'm not wrong about this, too." I picked up the beer and took a drink. "God, this sucks."

A soft knock came to the door. "Housekeeping, Mr. Dunne," came a woman's soft, lilting voice.

Galen raised his eyebrows. "Sounds like a Brit. I didn't know we had any on staff here. Must be a new hire." He got up and went to open the door. "Hello, please come in, lass. I'm Galen Dunn, the owner of this fine property."

"Yes, sir, I know," she said with a shy smile. "I'm here to make up the spare bedroom. Mrs. Chambers has told me you came with an unexpected guest."

"I see." He stepped back to let the maid inside. She carried a set of sheets and went straight to the bedroom. Galen put his hand on her shoulder to stop her. "And your name is?"

"Oh, sorry, sir." She looked down at her name tag. "I'm Ariel Pendragon, sir. I was hired on last month. It's a pleasure to meet you. I'll get to my work so I can get out of your way. I'm sorry about this."

"Don't be." Galen smiled at her, then came to sit back down as she left the room. "And take your time, Ariel. You're not in our way at all." He leaned back and looked at me. "Pretty little thing, isn't she? And what a lovely name, too. Ariel Pendragon. Nice, huh?"

I saw the look in his eyes. "Watch yourself, man. That's how it all started with me."

He laughed like there was no way in the world he would ever fall victim to love. "Not me, lad. Not me."

"I used to say the same thing, Galen." I took another drink. "Now look at me."

"Yes, look at you." He looked me over. "You don't look a thing like yourself, Astor. A T-shirt, blue jean shorts, tennis shoes—you've never worn clothes like that. Why now?"

"I wanted to show Nova how relaxed and laid back I am now." I shoved my hand through my hair. "It didn't do me any good, though. Nova didn't even make a single remark about my new look. I thought for sure she would say something about it. Maybe I don't really know her the way I thought I did."

"Could be." Galen's eyes traveled back to the door as another knock sounded.

Before he could get up, the maid came running out to answer the door. "I'll get it, sir." She opened the door, and a man stood there with our food on a cart. "Come in. You can put the food on the table, and I'll take care of the rest," she said.

Galen's eyes were glued to the young woman. "Thank you, Ariel."

I had to laugh, then whispered, "You know she's like twenty, right?"

His eyes came to meet mine. "And your point is?"

All I could do was shake my head and smile. "Nothing. No point, Galen." The girl was only about twenty or so years younger than him, but I guess he didn't see a problem with that.

I wondered if I'd have done things differently when I came to the island a year ago had I known how things would turn out. Falling in love is the perfect way to describe the experience. I'd never taken the time to think about why people called it *falling*. But now that I had first-hand experience, I understood it completely.

It's like you're standing on the edge of a cliff, minding your own business, then you see someone at the bottom of that cliff and all you can think about it getting to them. You jump. You fall—and continue falling. And it never ends.

And you can't turn it off, either. I could no more stop loving Nova than I could stop breathing. She could be furious with me and that didn't matter. I still loved her. She could tell me that she couldn't be with me all she wanted, but I'd still love her.

Once you fall, you can't stop.

"Maybe I've been going about this totally wrong, Galen." I got up and went to look out the window. His bungalow was inland, not an overwater one like the one I'd stayed at last year.

I could see people walking around outside. Lots of smiling faces. Lots of couples walking arm in arm or holding hands. And there I stood, watching them and feeling only love in my heart for Nova. And loneliness, too, since I was finally near her again, and she wanted nothing to do with me.

"Are you coming up with a new tactic, Astor?" he asked me.

"I've got to." I turned around to look at him. "I need to show her that I'm serious. Maybe the whole casual thing was a terrible idea. I've always been a serious man. She needs to be reminded of that."

"Your lunch is ready, sirs," the housekeeper announced.

I hadn't even noticed that the delivery boy had left. "Good, I need to eat and gather myself for my next move."

Galen and I took seats opposite one another at the table and once again he gave his attention to the pretty young maid. "Would you care to join us, Ariel?"

"Thank you, sir." She shook her head. "But I've got so much work to get to. It's kind of you to ask, though."

Galen seemed a little displeased that she wouldn't be joining us. "Okay then."

She left us, and I watched him watching her walk away. "I suppose it's her accent," he mumbled.

"And you say that because?" I asked as I cut into my steak, which had been cooked perfectly.

"No reason." He cracked his lobster claws, switching his attention to it, instead of the pretty maid. "So, what are you going to do next with Nova?"

"Back to the basics, I think." I popped a piece of meat into my mouth, and it nearly melted. "Man, that chef is good."

"He is," Astor agreed. "And by basics, what do you mean?"

My glass had been filled with red wine, which I picked up and took a drink of before going on, "What are the basic things to make women feel secure in their relationships?"

He shrugged. "Hell if I know the answer to that, Astor."

He wouldn't be any help at all, I could see. "Well, first of all, a woman wants to know that she's loved. I've let Nova know that much already."

"I would say that you have accomplished that much, yes." He took a bite of the lobster and moaned with satisfaction. "Oh, this is beyond delicious. They need to make a new word for what this is."

The food was good, and it was giving me the strength I needed to focus on winning my woman back. "So, what does a woman expect to come next, after knowing they're loved?"

"Marriage, I suppose." Galen lifted his glass. "Will I have a wedding to attend soon, my friend?"

I hadn't told him about my plan to ask Nova to marry me. "I've brought my great-grandmother's wedding set with me. But I want to wait until just the right time to ask Nova to marry me. I had all kinds of ideas about how to do it. But all of those ideas relied on the woman agreeing to be with me. And that's not going to happen anytime soon, it seems."

"Maybe you shouldn't rush into this, then." Galen shook his head. "Definitely don't rush this, Astor. I know I wouldn't."

"Yes, but you don't ever want to get married, Galen." I saw the maid walking out of the bedroom out of the corner of my eye.

She stopped dead in her tracks looking like she might have wanted to say something, but turned away instead, heading back to the bedroom.

"*You* might not," I said then took another drink, asking myself one last time if I was making the right choice. The answer was yes; I knew exactly what I wanted. "But I do want to get married. And I'm not going to sit back and hope Nova will come to her senses any longer."

Galen shook his head. "My advice is to give her time."

I'd already given her close to a year; I didn't know if I could stand being apart from her for much longer.

29

NOVA

M y head pounded with the worst headache of my life as I sat at my desk, trying in vain to get some work done.

I rubbed my temples, hoping to ease the pain a bit. I didn't want to take anything since I was breastfeeding. I didn't want any kind of pharmaceutical, even something as simple as an aspirin, coming out in my milk and going into my baby.

I'd stopped by the daycare and fed Mia after leaving Astor. It had helped me calm down for a little while, just bonding with my daughter. But when I left her and went back to work, all I could do was think about the fact that Astor was here on the island. And I felt stuck, like a bear with its foot in a trap.

Someone would tell him about Mia; it would only be a matter of time. I had to figure out a way of telling him first. But I didn't want to deal with the backlash of all that.

Astor would be furious with me for keeping that secret. And I had no idea what that would mean for me. But I was pretty sure that he would hate me, once he found out the truth.

After all the time I'd waited to hear him tell me that he loved me, and now he finally had. He'd said it over and over again. But I just knew that after he found out what a liar I'd been, he would never say those words to me again.

I'd messed up royally. And I had no idea how to fix it.

Camilla strolled into my office, wearing a smile. "I heard the news." She closed the door behind her. "Did you tell him yet?"

"Hell, no." I propped my elbows on the desk then rested my forehead in my hand. "Camilla, I don't know what to do."

She took a seat on the other side of my desk. "Um, you tell the man he's a father." She laughed. "It's simple, really."

I looked at her, trying to make her see the reality of the situation. "Camilla, he's going to hate me. He told me that he loves me. I've wanted to hear him say that for such a long time. And now, he's going to hate me, and he'll never say those words to me again."

She merely shrugged. "I doubt that."

I shook my head, wishing I could believe her. She had no idea how Astor really was. "I don't doubt it at all. He never wanted a kid. He told me so. And what did I do? I went and had his baby anyway."

"It's not like you did that on purpose, Nova," she reminded me. "Tell him the truth about everything."

All I could do was stare at her. "I don't know." My head was a mess. "And you know what makes me feel the worst?"

"What?" she asked.

"He told me that he loved me, and I couldn't say those words back to him. But I do love him." I felt horrible about that. "How can I tell him that I love him when I know what I tell him next will make him hate me?

"Look, you're overthinking this." She patted the back of my hand, which lay on the desk. "He's not some kid. Astor Christakos is a grown man. He was as aware of the potential consequences of a sexual relationship as you were." She waved her hand in the air. "You've got to get rid of all this anxiety and tell him already. Go get that beautiful baby girl, carry her to her father, put her in his arms, and tell him, *congratulations, this is Mia, your daughter.*"

"You make it sound so easy, Camilla." I knew it wasn't. "Besides, there's no way I can tell him like that. If he gets mad and yells at me, he'll scare the baby. I can't have her seeing us fighting like that." I knew I couldn't do what Camilla suggested, but I knew I had to tell him.

If he found out from someone else, he would hate me even more.

She got up, looking at me with a severe expression. "Whatever way you tell him, you know it's better than the alternative. It'd be awful for him to hear it from someone else first. If you hope to have any kind of future with that man—for your daughter's sake if nothing else—then you need to be the one to tell him. Plus, you're head over heels in love with him, and that means you've got to just stand up, take your licks—if you have any coming—and get on with this. The worst he can do is tell you that he's upset with you."

"Kyle said something about chaining me up and whipping me." I shuddered.

"You're not under that contract, my dear," she reminded me as she opened the door to leave my office. "He can't do that to you unless you let him. Do the right thing, Nova. You know what you've got to do now."

She closed the door, leaving me to think of all the ways he could punish me that didn't involve whipping me. His words could definitely hurt me just as badly.

My door opened again, and in a swift motion, Astor came in and closed it behind him. He'd changed out of his shorts and T-shirt and into a beige linen suit, looking more like the man I'd come to love a year ago. "Astor?"

"No talking." He came to me, pulling me up out of my chair. "Not a word until you are asked a question. Or you will face dire consequences."

That was fine with me. The words I had to say would only make him mad at me anyway. So I nodded.

He took both of my hands in his and then got down on one knee. My head swam.

"Nova, I have never known love until I met you," he began as he looked up at me with those gorgeous sea-green eyes. "I thought my life was so full that I could never fit you into it. I was wrong. There's room for you—plenty of it. Because you're a part of me now. It's become the most important thing in my life to make room for you. I've done little else, other than think about how we can live our lives together while still following our passions. I know you and I can do this, Nova. And I don't want you to be my summer fling or my long-distance girlfriend. I want you to be my wife. Marry me, Nova. Make me happier than I've ever been." He took a deep breath, looking vulnerable for the first time since he'd barged into my office. "So, what do you say? You can speak now."

I bit my lower lip as I thought about what I should say. "I love you, Astor. I really do. I understand now why you didn't contact me. I'm not mad about that anymore."

"Nova, why aren't you answering me?" His Adam's apple bobbed in his throat, and his eyes looked worried.

"You'll see why in a minute." I squeezed his hands. "I'm not mad, but I am afraid."

He shook his head. "You have nothing to be afraid of. I promise you that. I love you. I will always love you. You will be my number one priority. Work will be second."

He thought that now, but he didn't know we already had someone else that would have to put first,—before everything else. "Astor...that might not be possible."

"It will be possible. I will show you." He paused as he squeezed my hands. "Answer me, Nova."

I couldn't answer him yet. He had to know it all before I said anything else. "Astor, the idea of marrying you is so tempting. But I've got things going on in my life that you need to know about and that you need to take into consideration before you offer me marriage. You might not want to marry me after I tell you what I have to say."

He stared into my eyes, confused. "Have you been keeping some-thing from me, Nova?"

I nodded. "I have. And it may well affect your thoughts on marrying me. I want to say yes, but that wouldn't be fair to you."

He took a set of gold rings out of his pants pocket. "I want you to wear these. They were my great-grandmother's." He took me by the chin. "There's nothing that you can say that will make me change my mind about wanting to marry you. I can assure you of that." He smiled at me and then his lips barely touched mine as he whispered, "I love you so much. There is nothing in this world that can stop that love. I promise you that."

"Astor, I've done something you might find inexcusable." I pulled away from him, stepping back. "I've got to go now. But meet me in my bungalow in a half hour. Bring the rings if you'd like. But I doubt you'll want me wearing your great-grandmother's rings after you see what I've been keeping from you—what I thought to never tell you."

I walked away, unable to look back at him. The next time I saw his handsome face, I expected to see it contorted with rage.

30

ASTOR

Nova had left me feeling a little shell-shocked. She had a secret that she had thought to keep from me forever. I had to admit that I had not seen that coming.

I put the rings back into my pocket as I left her office. She'd told me to meet her at her bungalow in thirty minutes, but I had no idea which one was hers.

I walked down the hall until I found someone in an office. Camilla smiled at me as I stepped inside. "Hi, Astor. What a surprise to see you here. But a good one." She got up and hugged me. "Are you here looking for Nova?"

"I found her." I pulled the rings out of my pocket. "I asked her to marry me."

Camilla threw her hand over her mouth. "You did not! What did she say?" She looked at the rings in my hand. "Those are gorgeous. Are they antique?"

"They were my great-grandmother's, and Nova didn't really give me an answer. She said a lot of things. She said she'd like to marry me, but she said I needed to know something before she could give me a real answer." I looked at her, hoping she could help ease some of my confusion. "Do you know what she has to tell me, Camilla?"

"I might." She went back to take her seat behind the desk. "But you won't get a word out of me, Astor. What you will get is my sage advice."

"And that is?" I asked as I put the rings back into my pocket.

"Don't judge her too harshly," was all she said. "When did she say she was going to tell you?"

"In a half hour. She told me to meet her at her bungalow, but didn't tell me where it is." I shrugged. "Could you tell me that much, Camilla?"

"I can." She pointed at the back wall. "There are two bungalows just behind this building. Hers is on the right. Remember what I've said, Astor. Don't judge too harshly. If you love that girl enough to ask her to marry you, don't let this get in the way of that. It would be a real shame if you two lost the bright future you would have as a married couple if you let this change how you feel about her."

"How bad is it?" I had to ask.

"In my opinion, it's not bad at all." She smiled, then pointed to the door. "Go find out what it is. And I hope you two can make things work, Astor, I really do. Nova loves you very much."

"Well, at least I know it's not about her not loving me. That's something, I guess." I turned to leave and tried not to feel too anxious.

Sure, it felt like my life was hanging in the balance, but hopefully that feeling would soon pass. I would try my best to follow Camilla's advice and not judge too harshly. But it was damn hard to understand why she would say such a thing.

I went around the side of the building and saw one of the hosts walking up to the building. He waved at me and called out, "Astor, we should talk."

I'd seen the man around last year but couldn't recall his name. As he came up to me, I saw his name tag. "Hello, Kyle. It's nice to see you again. And what would you and I have to talk about?" I got the sick feeling it had to do with Nova, and then everything began to click. Kyle had been the host of my friends Grant and Isabel. And he was a Dom, too.

If he messed with her, there'd be Hell to pay.

The sound of Nova's voice made me turn around. "Astor, over here." She waved at me from the front door of her bungalow. "I forgot to tell you which one is mine." Her eyes flitted to Kyle, then back to me. "Come on."

I looked at Kyle. "What do we need to talk about, Kyle?" I had to know if they'd done anything before I heard a word she had to say to me.

"It looks like Nova's got a handle on it." He waved at her. "Proud of you," he called out to her.

She nodded. "Thanks."

I had no idea what the hell was going on, but I was about to get to the bottom of it. I walked toward her, though it might be more accurate to say I jogged. "Whatever you want to tell me, it seems like the whole island already knows. I hope you're done making me wait for an explanation, Nova."

"You won't have to wait another second." She stepped back to let me in, and I went inside and stopped in my tracks.

In the middle of the living room there was a small swinging basket. And inside of that basket lay a baby. "What's this?" I looked at Nova. "Are you babysitting?" I went inside, sure that had to be it.

She closed the door. "I am not babysitting. Her name is Mia."

Not sure what the hell was going on, I walked over to look at the little girl. She had dark hair, and her eyes were closed as she slept. "She's cute. Whose baby is she?"

"Yours." Nova came up to stand next to me. "Ours."

My heart stopped beating for a second, and I swear the world stood still as I repeated what she said in my head. "Ours?" I finally said aloud. I felt as if I was dreaming. "This can't be real."

"It's real, alright." Nova took my hand, pulling me to look at her. "Astor, I took a pregnancy test that day you left, when I went back to my room to put those things away. I was puking in the kitchen when Kyle came in. For some reason, the guy has a bunch of pregnancy tests, and he gave me one. That's when I found out I was pregnant."

"You knew before I left?" I couldn't believe it.

"I did." She looked down, and I could tell she felt ashamed. "I didn't want to tell you that I'd messed things up. You'd just told me that you had no time for a girlfriend or a child. I didn't know what to do."

My heart began to beat hard in my chest, and I pulled her into my arms. "You must've been so afraid." I held her tight and kissed the top of her head.

"I was out of my mind with fear." She looked up at me with tears in her eyes. "I thought that if you called me, then that would be fate telling me to tell you about the pregnancy. But you never called. But I'm not blaming you. I'm just telling you what I was thinking back then. How I tried to justify not telling you."

"I knew throwing that piece of paper into the ocean was a mistake. I kicked myself over and over again for doing that." Even though Nova said she didn't blame me, I couldn't help but blame myself a little. "This wasn't something you should've had to deal with alone. I'm sorry for that. But you could've told Camilla, and she would've told Galen, and he would've told me."

"I know that." She looked back down. "I just didn't want to ruin your life. If you called, then that meant you loved me. If you didn't, then I didn't want to burden you with a baby you never wanted. That's what I told myself. And I'll understand if you don't want anything to do with either of us now. I am sorry, Astor. I truly am."

I felt responsible for all of it. Every last thing. And the fact that she'd been planning to keep this baby a secret from me forever did hurt me. But not in the way she feared it would. It hurt me because it made me realize how much damage I'd done by leaving without letting her know how much I'd come to love her.

Lifting her face, I kissed her sweet lips. "I want you both, Nova. You're both mine to love and to take care of. I want you both. Say you'll marry me, and we can be a family."

She looked like she couldn't believe what I'd said. "Astor, you did hear me, right? I was never going to tell you about her. Not ever. Aren't you furious with me about that?"

"No." I swayed with her in my arms. "I'm mad at myself for not letting you know that I loved you before I left, for not showing you that I would always take care of you. I'm mad at myself for leaving the woman I loved. I'm mad that I threw your number away. But I'm not even a little mad at you, Nova. Not even a little."

She blinked as if she couldn't believe it. "This isn't how I thought you would react."

"I hope you're glad about that." I ran my hands down her arms and then pulled her left one up. "If you will finally answer the question I've asked you twice now, I would love to slip this engagement ring on your finger now."

With a sob, she burst into tears and nodded wildly. "Yes! Yes, I would love to marry you, Astor Christakos! I've loved you for so long! And I will never love anyone the way I love you! I will marry you!"

Her outburst had woken the baby, and the baby began to cry. I put the ring on Nova's finger and kissed her before turning to my daughter. "There, there, little one." I looked at Nova. "What did you say her name is?"

"Mia." She wiped her eyes and turned away to get a tissue. "I gave her my last name, but we can change it."

I picked my daughter up for the first time, and she felt so light in my hands. "You barely weigh a thing, Mia." She quit crying as soon as she heard my voice and looked straight at me. My whole world shifted with that one glance. "She has my eyes," I said in wonder.

"And your hair." Nova came back to my side, slipping her arm around my back. "She reminds me so much of you. I was thankful to have her."

I found that a little surprising. "You never thought about not keeping her?" My heart ached at the mere thought as I cradled my daughter in my arms.

"Not once. I knew I was getting to keep a part of you forever, and that made me happy. I've never loved anyone the way I love you." She kissed my cheek and then sighed. "And now I've got it all—you, our daughter. I couldn't ask for more." She held her hand out to look at the ring on her finger. "This ring is gorgeous. I just can't believe it."

"Believe it." I put my arm around Nova and carried our daughter to go sit down on the sofa. "We're a family. I've got a family." I laughed. "I came for a wife, and I got a whole family. How lucky can one man get?"

Nova rested her head on my shoulder. "How lucky can one woman get?"

"We will make this work. I don't want you to worry about a thing." I kissed Nova on the cheek. "But we will have to go to Greece. My family will want to meet you both."

"And I want to meet them," she gushed. "I can't wait!"

"My mother wants us to have the wedding there—if you're okay with that. I'll fly your family in for the occasion. I want to marry you as soon as possible." I looked down at the baby in my arms. "And I want to have lots and lots of babies, too. Brothers and sisters for our little Mia." I couldn't believe how much love spilled out of my heart for my girls.

Nova was on board with getting married in Greece, "Nothing would make me happier than getting married in your home, Astor."

We'd found it. In the middle of the Caribbean Sea, we'd found a slice of paradise and lots and lots of love.

The End

Did you like this book? Then you'll LOVE Tragic Secrets: Island of Love Series Book 2

It was supposed to be a time of mourning, reflection, and endings. Instead I found love, happiness, and new beginnings...

She'd caught my eye right from the start.
That little filly was as wild as they come, though.
Friends. That was her favorite word.
I wanted more, and I always get what I want.
But with her, love had to come first.
Her virginity meant a lot to her.

She meant a lot to me.
And just as it started coming together, it all came crashing down.
Why, I didn't know.
We were in love.
Or had it all just been a crazy game to her?

Start Reading Tragic Secrets NOW

**If you want to read the complete Island of Love Series you can get
your copy from your favorite bookstore here:**

Bad Boy Billionaire Romance Series: Island of Love Box Set

ABOUT THE AUTHOR

Mrs. Love writes about smart, sexy women and the hot alpha billionaires who love them. She has found her own happily ever after with her dream husband and adorable 6 and 2 year old kids. Currently, Michelle is hard at work on the next book in the series, and trying to stay off the Internet.

"Thank you for supporting an indie author. Anything you can do, whether it be writing a review, or even simply telling a fellow reader that you enjoyed this. Thanks